THE NINTH HOUR

THE NINTH HOUR

VALERIE VAN KOOTEN

PUBLISHING + DESIGN

Print ISBN: 978-1-7345829-4-9
Library of Congress Control Number: 2021904288

Published in the United States of America by the Write Place, Inc. For more information, please contact:

the Write Place, Inc.
809 W. 8th Street, Suite 2
Pella, Iowa 50219
www.thewriteplace.biz

Cover and interior design by Michelle Stam, the Write Place, Inc.
Cover stock image by Fon nayapan, shutterstock.com.

Scriptures taken from the Holy Bible, New International Version®, NIV®. Copyright © 1973, 1978, 1984, 2011 by Biblica, Inc.™ Used by permission of Zondervan. All rights reserved worldwide. www.zondervan.com. The "NIV" and "New International Version" are trademarks registered in the United States Patent and Trademark Office by Biblica, Inc.™

This is a work of historical fiction. While some of these characters and the situations they are in existed, their conversations are fictional. Other characters are totally the product of the author's imagination.

View other Write Place titles at www.thewriteplace.biz.

- SHOSHANNAH -

Shoshannah leaned out the window, pushing back the drapery that kept her bedroom in perpetual twilight. She looked out at the dusty road winding from her front courtyard. Through the grove of olive trees, she could see sheep in the small pasture. They would need to be sheared soon, as the days were growing increasingly warm. She remembered accompanying her father to the shearing when she was a small girl. She'd watch the shepherds, hired for the week, as they cradled the creatures' backs against their stomachs. The sheep would flail their legs in the air as they railed against their fate. After the initial struggle, they became resigned— no longer bleating or making any outcry, just waiting until it was all over.

Shoshannah could relate. Tomorrow evening, her groom would come and take her to the home he had been building so steadfastly, so quietly, over the past year. Her sisters constantly flounced in and out of her room, piling up linens and veils, offering pieces of their own jewelry for her neck and arms, making silly jokes about Ezra's handsome features and qualities as a husband. Shoshannah felt as if she were watching the whole tableau from someplace outside herself. When all was said and done, she was not so different from those suffering sheep. She, too, would bow her head to fate.

"Shoshannah, are you taking this pot with you tomorrow night, or will you return for it later? Mother wants to know!" Hannah, her ten-year-old sister, peeked into the room, a deep brown pot held aloft and her nutmeg-colored hair bouncing around her shoulders. "And are you wearing the silver earrings or the gold ones?"

"The gold ones, pet," Shoshannah replied, shaking herself from her reverie to answer her favorite sister. "And as for the pot, have Mother send it over in a day or two."

Hannah sped back down the steps, eager to help Shoshannah get her belongings in order. The whole house was in an uproar, sorting pottery, washing and pressing all the bride's clothing for the feast, making sure the entire family had new garments. So much to-do for something so dreaded, though Shoshannah knew she must put on her best face so no one guessed her true feelings.

As she turned from the window, she revised that statement. *Mother* knew. Mother knew her soul was dead to this marriage but then ... what else could have been done? As the matriarch constantly reminded her daughter, Shoshannah had brought this on herself.

Shoshannah fingered the veil she would wear, a veil she had embroidered with her own hands. She was known among the women of the community for her gifts of sewing and embroidery. The older women often warned her that stitches so small would cause her to go blind, but Shoshannah just laughed at them, proud of her work. Her family would never want for clothing, and they would have more than just the serviceable, practical things most people wore. Her husband's and children's clothes would be exquisitely sewn and decorated.

A husband. Children.

Funny how loving someone can bring such destruction, Shoshannah remonstrated with herself.

How could her love for Nathaniel have brought her to this? Was there any way it could have ended differently? She pulled the drapery closed behind her, shut the door to her room, and lay down on her pallet. She felt a headache coming on, and she needed to think clearly before it claimed her entire body.

Nathaniel … brilliant. Clever. Hair like burnished bronze. Of all the boys who clambered around her after synagogue services—bringing her candies, offering her small gifts, wandering to her home on transparent errands—only Nathaniel had caught her attention. He was aloof, self-assured. And he'd had set his sights on Shoshannah. The thought of his gaze and the first time he'd spoken to her—"Will you permit me to ask your father if I may call on you some evening?"—still turned her stomach to water.

Nathaniel had come to dinner many evenings. He was always served the best meals her mother could conjure up—

braised fish on open coals, roast lamb, tabbouleh, fresh figs. As time passed, her father's instincts to chaperone his beautiful daughter wore down, and Shoshannah and Nathaniel were increasingly allowed to wander through the olive grove in front of the house alone.

Nathaniel talked of many things Shoshannah did not understand, but she always listened with interest and tried to learn from him—the ways of the planets and stars; how the wind swept across the desert and through the verdant valley where they lived; what caused the locusts to swarm through the villages, as if they had an inner clock that guided them all at the same time. Shoshannah marveled at Nathaniel's knowledge of the ways of the natural world, of his recognition of the Creator's grand designs.

These evenings never ended with anything more scandalous than a caress of the cheek, or a brief meeting of the lips. Until the night Nathaniel threw down his cloak and they lay on the green tussocks of the grove to drink in the black velvet that was the Judean night sky. As they lay there, quiet, breathing in the scent of honeysuckle that wafted across the breeze, Shoshannah felt Nathaniel's hand brush the side of her thigh. She became paralyzed with desire, not daring to breathe or believe what she was feeling. When he pushed himself up on one elbow and looked in her eyes, she knew that whatever he asked of her, whatever he took from her, she could not deny him. She would rather have cut out her own heart than say no to him.

When she stumbled back into the house an hour later, she headed straight to her room, hoping to reach its safety before her parents saw her. But it was too late. As she reached the foot of the stairs, her mother walked out from the kitchen, holding a mixing bowl under her arm and a spoon in her hand. Their eyes met, and Shoshannah knew her mother had seen her—seen not only the depths of her soul, but also the grass stains on her skirt, her askew veil, her overly reddened lips and cheeks. Her mother knew. After all, her mother knew everything. Shoshannah continued to stare brazenly into the older woman's eyes, daring her to say anything, and her mother was the first to retreat. She quietly bowed her head and returned to the kitchen.

After that night, a perplexing thing happened. At first, Shoshannah's heart sang with love and generosity. She laughed with her little sisters and played the games they loved that she'd told them she'd outgrown. Her family saw the glow emanating from the tawny-haired girl. Her tall, lithe frame often danced through the grove.

"Shoshannah's in love," they all muttered with the wisdom of the ages, and her father started calculating what a wedding would cost him in terms of a dowry. Only Shoshannah's mother watched with veiled eyes and a heavy heart.

But Nathaniel suddenly disappeared from the picture. When he did not return for several nights, Shoshannah assumed he was busy in his family's milling business. When several more days went by, she worried he might be sick but was too proud to send a messenger to tell her. After three weeks with no word from him, Shoshannah realized Nathaniel was not coming back.

He did not want her.

Shoshannah's mother was the first to make the next dreaded discovery. She monitored the monthly cycles of the women of the household using the laundry that came through her hands, so she was the first to notice Shoshannah had missed her time of blood. *But surely these things happen to young girls,* she convinced herself. Often their cycles were not as regular as the moon. When a second month passed without soiled undergarments being placed in the rag basket to be cleaned, Shoshannah's mother marched up the steps to confront her daughter.

Oh, it was ugly, ugly. Shoshannah remembered it all as she tossed onto her right side. Her mother had accused her of being nothing better than a harlot, of giving herself away cheaply to the first boy who looked at her. Shoshannah would not hear those things about Nathaniel. Even though he had broken her heart, he still held it in his hands. She would not allow her mother to turn something so beautiful into filth. She would hear nothing about Nathaniel that was not honorable, and she'd told her mother so.

"*Honorable?*" her mother's scream pierced the air. "What about him is *honorable*? He has used you and left you with child! Do you realize what this will mean in the synagogue? Do you realize you will have *no* marriage prospects?"

Shoshannah had buried her head under her pillow, fighting the rising nausea that choked her. What in the name of Elohim would she do now—the same Elohim Creator who had fashioned men and women for love and passion?

For two months she wandered the house like a wraith, interested in nothing, not even her prized embroidery. Her wan face haunted the younger children, who did not understand why Shoshannah no longer wanted to play games or go on walks with them. Her father, embarrassed by the whole situation, retreated to corners of the house, where he had heated conversations with her mother. Shoshannah had overheard them many times.

"You must go to the elders at the city gate and demand recompense," her mother would hiss.

"Then her disgrace will be in the open for all to see. I would rather die," he would retort.

"Everyone's going to see it anyway ... and soon. Should we send her away? What if the elders want to stone her?"

And so the arguments raged, but never in front of Shoshannah. Only in whispers, in bits of conversation caught as she turned a corner. *What to do with Shoshannah?* It became the all-consuming focus of the house.

Shoshannah lay on her back, eyes wide open, remembering those miserable two months. She had become a burden to the family, a disgrace, an embarrassment. But in His mercy, Hashem had sent the solution. One morning, as Shoshannah awoke and rose from her pallet to get dressed, a cramp doubled her, and a gush of bright red blood poured from between her legs. Shoshannah screamed for her mother, who rushed into the room and, after assessing the situation, breathed, "The Almighty be praised!" Then she pushed Shoshannah back down and rushed around, gathering towels and warm water.

And so ended the *problem*, at least in her parents' eyes.

Now Shoshannah listened to the bustle downstairs. The sounds of pans being replaced on the high shelf after washing, her sisters playing a game outdoors with a ball they bounced repeatedly against the house, a donkey being brought in for the night. Although the problem of an illegitimate child had been solved, the problem of Shoshannah's broken spirit had not. She simply was not herself. Her mother watched her, plied her with potions of herbs and broths that would bring back her strength, set her to work on a complicated sewing project that required all her concentration. And though Shoshannah obeyed with perfect compliance, her heart was not in anything and her mother knew it.

One evening, as she sat at the fire and sewed, her father sat down heavily next to her in the chair at the hearth. This was unusual, as he was almost always outdoors in the barn until dark. Shoshannah knew there must be something weighty on his mind.

He succinctly laid out his plan. Shoshannah would be betrothed to Ezra, from the family of Naahum. Her father had approached Ezra himself and struck a bargain. Ezra knew of the situation but would keep it to himself. He had promised Shoshannah's father to take care of her and treat her with love and respect. The wedding would take place in a year, time that Shoshannah would spend getting ready by filling her chest with all the things a bride needed. Her father would provide a fitting dowry for the daughter of a wealthy landowner.

And then her father sat back, relieved a solution had been found, that all the loose ends had been tied up. Shoshannah was too numb to reply and could only nod vaguely.

"So it's settled then," her father said, rising, slapping his meaty hands against his thighs in relief.

Settled? Shoshannah thought. *What is settled for you is the beginning of the end for me.*

The next months found Shoshannah in forced and awkward conversations with Ezra, always under the watchful eye of one of her parents or with all the younger children underfoot. They exchanged polite words, and Shoshannah accepted the small gifts Ezra brought her—a cedarwood jewelry box he had carved, a fine piece of wool dyed crimson, a perfectly smooth rock the color of a bird's egg. In return, Shoshannah threw herself into her sewing, making Ezra a sash that was the envy of the men at the synagogue, fine stitches depicting King David and his battle with the giant Goliath.

And all the while, as she talked in stilted terms with Ezra, she sensed he had his own sorrows, that he was keeping something from her. But she didn't hold it against him. After all, when could they discuss anything privately, with the whole horde of her family constantly in the way? Let Ezra have his secrets and his heartbreak. Shoshannah would keep hers to herself. It was better that way.

Tomorrow she would smile, she would dance, and she would say all the right things to her family and friends. No one needed to know what she really felt. No one needed to know her shame and emptiness.

- LILITH -

There was no way on earth everything would be ready by two days past the next Sabbath—the first day of the wedding feast. There were mountains of bread to bake, extra pots and olive oil vats to keep track of, wine that would be delivered…

Lilith still wasn't sure that donkey-brained wine vendor could be trusted. Hadn't he brought total disgrace to the son of her neighbor, Shira, last year when he didn't deliver enough? Ever since old Jeremiah had succumbed to the pain in his joints and given the business over to his flea-brained son, disaster had followed. She would make a note to have her husband, Naahum, double-check the wine order and threaten a hearing with the elders at the city wall, physical beatings, public disgrace …whatever it took to be sure the wine was superb and plentiful.

Oh, these servant girls would be the death of her, too. Here came one carrying a load of laundry too heavy for her, with half the sun-whitened sheets dragging on the ground. They would have to be re-washed, and there simply wasn't time for mistakes. Just yesterday, another hired girl had broken the flour pot she'd borrowed from her neighbor, Mariah—the old hag—and now she would have to put considerable expense into replacing it *and* bow in shame in front of the gossipy old hex. No more mistakes, not when half the province would be descending on the house of Naahum to celebrate the marriage of their son, Ezra, and Shoshannah, the stunning girl who'd surprised them all by accepting his bid for marriage.

Shoshannah—"lily," even her name was musical—had an impeccable pedigree. That a girl who traced her heritage to the tribe of Naphtali—the tribe that had spawned princes in the prophet Isaiah's time—would consent to marry Ezra was a step up for the whole family.

Not, of course, that their family had to hang its head. Naahum had done well for himself in the wool trade, buying from the nomads in the fields surrounding Cana, then processing and dyeing the wool and selling it to be woven into the fine tunics and robes worn by the upper class. No, she could find no fault in Naahum. He was a good man, a steady man, though a little dull and unimaginative. She saw the same traits in her Ezra—a fine, dependable boy, though she wasn't sure he had the charisma to hold Shoshannah. Girls like her new daughter-in-law wanted adventure and romance, and Lilith wasn't sure the men of her family could deliver. Naahum certainly hadn't, Hashem forgive her. Pray to the Almighty Shoshannah would remain faithful to her son.

Lilith sighed, then shrugged, as if shaking off her misgivings. Of course she would be faithful. Shoshannah was from a God-fearing family and knew her role as a proper wife. Rumor had it her handwork—her embroidery and sewing—were exquisite and surpassed that of other girls her age. Perhaps she could make a little money of her own on the side. That would satisfy most women, give them some independence. That would settle her down. After all, hadn't Lilith herself come into her union with doe eyes and unrealistic expectations of what married life would be like? And hadn't she been abruptly dragged out of that dream when the real world of work and children and in-laws intruded? Of course her son's marriage would be fruitful and blessed.

When Lilith thought about the bride Ezra had originally wanted, she shuddered. No, she had to be honest—there had been nothing wrong with the girl herself. They had met her only once, when Ezra had had the temerity to bring her into their home. Quiet, meek, and pretty in an ordinary sort of way—Lilith had seen in her the makings of an obedient daughter-in-law and a submissive wife. She'd moved quietly, gracefully, her jet-black eyes taking everything in and learning quickly. She'd seldom spoken, but when she had, her gentle humor had been appealing.

But the match was unthinkable. She was a *Samaritan*, a half-breed, a reject of the true faith.

Lilith tried to banish the memory of the subtle warfare that had followed—the hissed arguments in corners of the house, the tension that trailed Ezra out to the barn, where she and her husband would corner him and try to talk sense into him. The slamming doors, and the bewildered younger children who knew something was desperately wrong but didn't know what it was. A black blanket of melancholy had lain over the household for several months.

In those dark days, Lilith had seen the first sparks of spirit in her otherwise phlegmatic son—he'd argued that times were changing, that Melea (even her name was foreign and strange!) would convert to true Judaism, that she was who he wanted for a bride. But Lilith and Naahum had stood firm. As much as they loved their son and wanted his happiness, the marriage was impossible. They would be disgraced before their families and neighbors. They would lose business. Their bloodlines would be tainted. If Ezra followed this foolish and ill-advised path, he would be cut off from the family with no contact, no support, no inheritance.

One evening, at the conclusion of the Sabbath—after dinner was finished and his sisters were carefully wrapping the leftover rice in large grape leaves to keep it fresh—Ezra approached his parents.

"It is done," he muttered in a dead voice. "I have sent Melea away, and I will see her no more."

Then he turned and walked out the door, shutting it quietly behind him. In that moment, Lilith felt a little piece of herself die for her son, even as a surge of relief ran through her veins.

But why was she dwelling on such dismal thoughts just a few days before this celebrated wedding feast? The Almighty had blessed her beyond measure to take her son's sadness and turn it to such joy. It had all happened so quickly—barely two months after the debacle with the Samaritan girl, Ezra had approached Naahum and asked him to go to Shoshannah's father to discuss terms of marriage. They had all been stunned—no one knew he'd even been visiting her.

Shoshannah, who had men swarming about her like flies around a honey pot.

Shoshannah, one of the most eligible girls in the countryside surrounding Cana.

The rumor mill said she was also being visited by Nathaniel, the firstborn son of the village miller. And she had chosen Ezra? It seemed unbelievable ... but who were they to question the ways of Hashem?

Ezra refused to discuss how he had met her or how the courtship had begun. He would only say that he wished to have Shoshannah for his wife, that he had good reason to believe she would consent. Would his father see to the arrangements?

It was a command, not a request. On this point, Ezra was adamant—he would not participate in the betrothal rituals. His father could negotiate a bride price, oversee the contract—the *ketubah*—and drink the binding toast with his betrothed's father. Naahum started to protest, to laugh, to convince his son that such a deal was never made without the bridegroom in attendance. But something in Ezra's eyes stopped him. And so the following evening, quietly and somewhat abashed, acknowledging a new authority in his son, Naahum had bathed, put on his best tunic and sandals, anointed his head with sweet-smelling lavender oil, and made the two-mile trek to the home of Shoshannah's father. Whether her father thought this a strange betrothal, with no groom in attendance, Naahum never said. Lilith never asked. Instead, she watched her son go through his days with a dead heart.

Almost a year had passed since that evening, a year in which Ezra dutifully built two rooms onto his parents' home for the new family he would form with his bride. A year in which Shoshannah prepared a dowry chest and gathered the necessary items for her new life—blankets, pots, pans, and textiles. As part of her bride price, her *mofar*, Naahum had offered Shoshannah's family a heifer, two ewes, and a ram. In a burst of generosity—*And he could certainly afford it,* Lilith thought—Shoshannah's father had good-naturedly given those animals to the young couple, though he kept the fine woolens and expensive nard for himself.

The year had passed quickly, with lists and dried goods to be tallied and pots to be borrowed. In the next week, Ezra would make his way to Shoshannah's home to collect her, with his friends and brothers in attendance. The men would stand underneath her window and call loudly and wildly for the bride to come down. Lilith thought of her own wedding feast with disgust. Several of Naahum's friends had already been drunk when they'd arrived at her house. They'd yelled inappropriate and vulgar things at her window. She hoped Ezra's childhood friends would have more sense than that.

In theory, of course, the actual date and time of the bride's collection were supposed to be a secret. But Shoshannah's entire family knew the score and would be ready to send their beautifully bedecked daughter onto the road with the groom and his party. They would then make their way back to Ezra's home, where the celebrations would begin.

And that was when Lilith's duties would commence. The servant girls would need to keep everyone happy, and she and Naahum would need to be impeccable hosts. Of course the food would be plentiful. And the wine—oh, even the wine for the feast was a tangible reminder of Ezra's first choice, for wasn't it coming from Samaria, as was most of the wine purchased in Galilee? Only a few jars of the more expensive (and better quality) Cyprian wine had been ordered. They would start with those and then—Hashem help her—bring out the Samarian wine as the guests became intoxicated. They wouldn't know the difference by then.

Glancing at the ground, Lilith discovered yet another piece of pottery from Mariah's broken flour pot. With a sigh, she bent to pick it up and move it to the junk heap—another thing that needed to be tended to before the wedding. She made a mental note to ask the hired man doing heavy work around the courtyard to have the pile of refuse taken away. The last thing the guests needed to see was trash and broken pots in the place where the feast would be held. There would be singing, dancing, and eating, with much suggestive joking thrown in—which the women would pretend they didn't understand.

Thanks to the Almighty some wedding customs have changed, she thought. When Lilith had married Naahum, the old customs still prevailed. Soon after arriving at Naahum's home, clad in her beautiful gold headpiece and dove-gray robes, she was escorted to the couple's new bedroom, undressed by her sisters and friends, then left alone in the large bed. The sounds of the musicians tuning up outdoors and the cries of her family and friends as they greeted each other had rung in her ears until Naahum, more than a little drunk, stumbled into the darkened bedchamber and stood there awkwardly.

By the gods, they had been children—she fourteen and Naahum sixteen—and Lilith still wanted to throttle her mother, though she had been dead for years, for how little she'd been told about this embarrassing and highly unromantic encounter. The memory of Naahum's excited fumbling and the pain that ensued blurred together ... and then he'd fled the bedchamber with their sheet. The bright drops of blood on snowy fabric proved she had, indeed, come to the marriage bed undefiled. Oh, the shame of it. Her face grew red at the thought. At least that backward, barbaric ritual had been replaced by a more dignified feast and celebration.

Lilith reminded herself to count the guests who would be coming. Naahum didn't have a large family—his brother, along with wife and children, would be there; Naahum's elderly mother would certainly attend, and she would have to have a servant girl assigned just to her to fetch her food and help her in and out of her chair; all of Lilith's sisters and brothers and their families would come, and they would have to be housed; and then, of course, her cousin, Mary, would be there. She hadn't seen Mary for two years, though their villages weren't that far apart. Mary was her favorite cousin, although she was quite a bit older than Lilith. Their fathers were brothers, and as a young girl, Lilith had followed Mary around like a pet lamb, wanting to brush her hair and anoint her feet. Mary must surely have seen her as a nuisance, though she'd never been anything but kind to the younger girl.

Mary's children would probably attend with their mother, now that Joseph was gone. So sad about the sudden fit that had taken him, but maybe it was for the best. Lilith had seen old men in the community taken with such fits, who later could only slobber with half their faces frozen stiff. They couldn't walk or control their bowels. Yes, it was better Joseph had passed quickly.

Lilith paused, her eyes glazing over as she remembered. She set down the mortar and pestle she was using to grind spices. That whole business of Mary and Joseph's marriage—it had been strange, and very few in her family would talk of it. Lilith had been too small to understand what was going on. Now, as an adult, she often pondered the situation. She knew Mary well enough to be certain she would not have slept with Joseph before the wedding feast. Not that Mary was a saint, and any girl could be overcome with desire when young blood was racing. But she had been very sheltered by her family. And Joseph—that man had been more patient than anyone Lilith had ever known. She just couldn't see Joseph forcing himself on Mary in the back of some cowshed.

Yes, the whole situation was quite odd. There was talk at the time of Mary's son being conceived by the Almighty One—preposterous, to be sure, and how the gossip and laughter had followed that rumor! There were those who thought Mary had been raped by one of the Syrian traders who came through their village; others even spoke shamefully of abuse within Mary's own household by one of her brothers.

The question of Yeshua's birth was certainly mysterious.

Lilith straightened and turned her attention back to her spices. She shrugged her aching shoulders back and forth. Yeshua would certainly come to the wedding, and a frown crossed Lilith's face at that thought. If Yeshua came, those undesirables who hung around him would probably be there as well.

Lilith didn't relish feeding a half dozen or so extra men who weren't related to the family and who were—yes, she would say it—*uncouth*. They were rough, unmannered—some of them fishermen. Lilith had only seen them once with Yeshua at the market in nearby Capernaum, but they'd struck her as strange, out of place. What were grown men doing gallivanting around the country? What did they see in Yeshua, Mary's son, to compel that sort of loyalty? Certainly Yeshua was a nice boy, an obedient boy, devoted to his family and helping support them now that Joseph was gone. But why couldn't he be a proper rabbi, teaching in a synagogue, sitting at the gate, and discussing Scripture? Why this need to tramp from one region to another, like a wandering bird with no nest?

Well, whatever her reluctance, Lilith would be sure her home was a beacon of hospitality, for Mary's sake if nothing else. She would welcome Yeshua and his followers, as well as the rest of her family and Naahum's family and the many friends and relatives who would descend on them.

Feeling new resolve, she again vowed to light a fire under Naahum to go after the wine vendor. Everything needed to be perfect for the feast of her son and his beautiful bride.

- Maret -

If one more neighbor stopped by to offer good wishes, press food on her family, or hand them bags of money to make sacrifices at the Temple, Maret thought she would fly into a storm of tears and call off the entire trip. Her nerves were tightly strung, and though she appreciated the blessings of her family and friends, she wanted to lock the doors and ignore the constant pounding and raised voices of greeting in her courtyard.

As she sat on the edge of her bed, shredding what remained of her right thumbnail with her left hand, Maret went over the trip once again in her mind. She and Simon had planned for this, saved for it, sat down in the evenings after the boys were in bed, and figured out how much money it would take, how far the route would be, and where they would stay. The detail had been painstaking, but always—*always*—as they'd pored over the papyrus scribblings, it had all seemed like a dream to Maret. It had never seemed like this journey would *actually* take place. Even now, less than one week before leaving, Maret still wasn't sure it wouldn't disappear like the mist that hung over the river in the early mornings.

She savored the coolness of the room as she counted the tunics once more, placing them in a large flax sack. The thick clay blocks of the house kept out the searing sun, and when she pulled the tapestries across the windows, the rooms stayed refreshing, even on the hottest days. Through her sandals, she could feel the dampness of the block floor—not an unpleasant feeling, but one that served to keep Maret's entire body cool.

She thought again of the days of travel ahead. The rudimentary maps they had of the journey from Cyrene to Jerusalem showed several larger rivers and streams, not to mention the mighty Nile, so she would not pack too much. She and Simon had planned days to stop and bathe, wash their clothing, and let the boys spend their restless energy exploring. They had also padded the schedule with a few extra days in case of emergencies—a crippled leg on their ass, sickness in the family, or swollen rivers that would need to recede before they could cross. If everything went as expected, they would be near Jerusalem just before the Passover.

Simon had no doubt they would meet other pilgrims on the road, with whom they could band together for safety. Until then, they would stick to the widely traveled roads, even if the shortcuts would bring them to their destination faster. They were carrying too much of their friends' and neighbors' money to be robbed. And that wasn't the worst of it. They had heard too many stories of bandits setting on decent, hard-working travelers, stripping them of their clothing and jewelry, beating them, robbing them, and leaving them for dead. They would take no chances.

Banishing her worries, Maret clutched her husband's blue tunic to her chest in a sudden fit of excitement and disbelief. To be traveling so far to celebrate the Passover in Jerusalem! But then her stomach lurched, and once again she toppled onto the edge of the bed. It was a dream for most of the Jews in their small village so close to the Egyptian border, a dream that would never come to life. Though observant Jews around the world wished to be part of the celebrations in Jerusalem at Passover, those in the far-flung countries away from Judea—like Maret and Simon and their boys in Cyrene—often saw the trip as a fantasy that would never happen. The expense, the time away, the pressing duties of children and work, would not allow it.

Maret hummed happily to herself—a weird, tuneless little ditty her father had often whistled. She knew if any man could make this journey happen, her Simon could. Steady, dependable, employed in a position of high prestige with the village elders—if her Simon said they would go to Jerusalem, she should have known it would happen. They knew only one other person who had made the trip—old Hamant from the nearby village, who had gone as a young man. The couple invited him over often, pulling every detail from him like a dog sucking marrow from a bone.

How many people could they expect to see once they came to Jerusalem?

How much food should they pack?

Should they plan on finding a room at an inn, or camp outside the city wall with other pilgrims?

What was the protocol for approaching the Temple and buying a sacrifice?

Hamant, wizened and approaching his ninetieth year, had recalled as many details as he could in his shaky voice, though he had the maddening habit of beginning a story of some consequence, then letting his mind meander down another path. Simon would politely but firmly coax him onto his original train of thought; from their many evenings together, Simon and Maret had gleaned the following.

The city of Jerusalem normally held about 60,000 citizens—a number too large for Maret to even comprehend—but it would swell to more than 150,000 people during the week before the Passover. They needed to bring as much food as they could, for prices would skyrocket. And they shouldn't even bother trying to find a place to stay in the city, unless they had friends or relatives there. Instead, they should camp outside the city with other bands of pilgrims, who would take turns staying behind and guarding each other's belongings.

Simon and Maret had heeded his advice, packing many dried foods—figs, dates, dried meat, barley, and wheat—as well as basic medicines that might be needed en route and a few changes of clothing. Their little ass would carry Maret when she grew too tired to walk, plus all their supplies.

Maret would also let the boys take a turn riding when they needed a break.

Oh, the boys—sick with excitement they were. For so long they had heard their parents planning this trip. They would roll their eyes in boredom as Simon took down the cracked papyrus rolls to figure once again what was needed and how far it would be.

Like Maret, the boys never thought it would truly happen. And so, the couple didn't tell them at first that this was the year. That yes, they were really going to Jerusalem. Maret had known that once the idea sunk in, their questions would be constant.

And she was right. Rufus, seven, and Alexander, ten, had looked at their parents, goggle-eyed, when they'd made the announcement. After bursting out the door to spread the news around the neighborhood, they'd bounded back into the kitchen.

Where would they sleep?

Who would take care of their lamb while they were gone?

Could they take the lamb along?

Would the synagogue school rabbi be angry they were missing so many classes?

Where would they go to the bathroom while traveling?

Simon, in his patient and direct way, had answered each question as seriously as if he had posed it himself. So dear he was, so considerate, even of his boys' eager and annoying interruptions. Just last night, he had sat down with Alexander after the meal and helped him draw a map of where they would go and what they would see. Three months, they figured. They would be gone almost three months.

And so much to do yet. Maret had made a mental list of everything that still needed to be washed, packed, and taken care of before they left. Her sister's children would come over to care for the family's animals. They were serious, earnest children and would not neglect their duties. Maret would finish the laundry tomorrow, washing and packing extra linen shifts for Rufus, who tended to pee into his bedclothes during the night.

Maret sighed. Neither the large spoonful of honey, the crushed basil in olive oil taken just before bedtime, nor the splash of vinegar in a small mug of water had stopped Rufus from wetting himself at night. She would need a way to store his wet clothes until she could get to a stream to wash them. Surely they would begin to stink.

There it was again—a pounding at the front door, another friend or neighbor to see them off. Truly, truly she was blessed to be so surrounded by those who loved them and were excited for them, but at that moment she wished all of them would stay away. It had become apparent soon after they'd announced their plans that they were taking this trip for the entire village. Not only were they expected to bring money to purchase sacrifices in their neighbors' names, they were being asked to purchase trinkets to bring back to the village. A piece of Capernaum lace. Salts from the Dead Sea. Lavender oil from the fields surrounding

Jerusalem. She and Simon were expected to deliver all the things the people of Cyrene had heard about, read about, dreamed about.

Maret stood up, put her arms to her thin back, and stretched. Her muscles were cramped. Tonight she would ask Simon to rub between her shoulders, where she could feel knots of muscle needing to be smoothed out. She headed to the front door, hoping whoever was there would move along, but the knocking continued.

She peeked through the drapery in the kitchen and quickly opened the door. It was Miriam, her mother's oldest friend, leaning against her walking stick. As the sun lit up her head from behind, Maret was struck by how old Miriam had become—Miriam, who was always so full of life, so vibrant! She had delivered both of Maret's sons with the ease of an experienced midwife, bringing calm and confidence to a panicked and pain-ridden girl. Her warm and loving nature made her a welcome guest in any household. Maret widened the door and urged her to come in.

"I know you are in the middle of so many preparations," Miriam began as she pushed herself into the room with her stick. Maret remembered Miriam's knee was going bad. "But I could not let you leave without asking for a small favor."

Maret grinned as she led the older woman to a stool by the fire. What would it be this time? She had better start a list of her friends' and neighbors' requests, or she would never be able to remember them all. Still, she would have no problem remembering anything Miriam asked of her.

"Do you want lavender oil, like our neighbors next door?" Maret asked. "Or maybe some fresh pomegranates from the Jordan?"

Miriam made an impatient gesture that showed her distaste for such things. "You should know me better than that! I do not wish for anything money would buy, but only a piece of the land of our people—a rock or a twig that comes from the land of our ancestors." Her eyes were earnest as she bent forward, grabbing Maret's hands with her own, brown-spotted and purple-veined. "I will never make the journey myself, but I wish to possess a piece of the place … something that has impressed you, so I can share its story."

Maret's liquid brown eyes twinkled with laughter. "Perhaps you are just too cheap to buy anything of significance," she said with a giggle. "A rock won't cost you much!"

Miriam joined her in a fit of girlish laughter. "Oh, you know me too well! You are right—I do not care much for the material things of this world, but truly, Maret … "

She leaned over and again grabbed the younger woman's wrist. "Bring me back something. You will know it when you see it."

"I promise I will bring you back something."

Maret jumped up to offer her guest mead and honey, along with watered-down wine, suitable for midday drinking. She was sure she still had some honey wafers in the cupboard, the ones she had baked several days ago, unless the boys had gotten into them and shared them with the neighborhood horde. Maret smiled to herself—the group of boys who hung around her door and the thresholds of her neighbors' houses were like a pack of wild dogs, always hungry, always getting into mischief. But no ... the honey wafers were still there, undisturbed.

"Ah, Maret," Miriam sighed as her hostess set the provisions in front of her. "You are the soul of hospitality, and I know how many things you have to do before you leave. And I've heard how many people are bothering you to buy them things. How will you ever get it all back home?" She adjusted the sash to her tunic, which tended to ride up on her short waist whenever she sat down.

"It is a bit much," Maret began, wincing a little. "Simon wants to spend as much time as possible at the Temple, but I think we'll spend two full days shopping!" Seeing a look of pity in the older woman's eyes, she leaned forward to reassure her. "Not that I begrudge it, not at all," she assured her. "We seem to be taking this trip for the village, not just ourselves. I realize this is a dream few in our area will ever see come true."

Miriam leaned forward and rubbed her sore knee. "Yes, and you are most generous, my child," she said. "Just don't forget to enjoy this trip for yourself, your husband, and your children. You will remember it the rest of your life."

Maret ran through the lists of food, clothing, and other provisions they were taking, making notes to add a few healing herbs to her list that Miriam suggested. Finally, as the sun began to work its way through the back window, Miriam heaved herself to her feet and made her way to the door.

"Adonai's blessings on you, my child," she said as she reached out to hug Maret. "Make a picture of all you see in your mind, so you can share it with your old friend Miriam."

As Maret watched Miriam hobble up the lane, she was again tempted to pinch herself to see if it were true. She, Maret of Cyrene—a village girl who had never been more than twelve furlongs from her place of birth—was journeying many, many miles away with her husband and two sons. She would face all sorts of adventures.

More important than all the items they were to buy, the clothing and provisions they were packing, the plans that had to be made before they could leave, was the thought of actually spending the Passover in Jerusalem. The City of David. The feast of deliverance. Celebrating with Jews from all over the world. Maret's heart began pounding as she pondered all that would mean.

She had an ineffable feeling of being chosen. She hoped they were worthy of the task.

- ISAAC -

Isaac woke with one thought on his mind. He sat up on his mat, wondering if it had been a dream, half hoping it were so.

Another child. His wife, Leah, had told him last night they would be bringing another life into the world in the autumn. "Praise be to the Almighty," he'd automatically murmured, all the while feeling a wave of nausea break across his throat and stomach. A *seventh* child. On a poor scribe's salary. He sank back onto his thin pillow and ran his long, slender fingers through his fuzzy, reddish-brown hair.

Another blessing … he smiled wryly. He knew Yahweh would provide. Of that, there had never been any doubt. But in the meantime, he could just hear his neighbors joking.

"Yahweh may provide, Isaac, but it would help to know what's causing it!"

Leah was already up and beginning breakfast; he could hear her poking the fire to life and gathering the pots for her trip to the well later that morning. Leah—his dove, the love of his life. How right the ancient writer who'd said a good wife's worth was beyond rubies. And how he desired her. Some husbands and wives kept separate beds, to avoid bringing any more children into the squalor and deprivation of poverty. Often they were in separate rooms too, with the man sleeping in the boys' bedroom and the woman in the girls'. He could never do that. He needed Leah as the land needed water in this parched country. So he sighed, offering yet another wry smile. If Adonai continued to send blessings, he would receive them, work for them, and care for them.

Isaac dressed quickly, pulling on his shift; his *tzitzit*, the fringed undergarment that reminded him of his constant devotion to God; and his outer tunic, much patched and darned, but always clean and smelling of the lavender that grew in the fields outside Jerusalem. He reached into the cupboard in the bedroom and pulled out his *tefillin*—those small boxes prescribed by Moses in Deuteronomy that contained snippets of the Torah. Isaac strapped them to his forehead and upper arms and began his morning prayers. This was what centered him. This should be his first thought each morning at waking and his last before drifting off to sleep. Isaac was ashamed of his worries and fears over the new life that would be joining his family.

He had six healthy children already—five robust, strapping boys and one daughter, his Leila. Perhaps Yahweh would favor them with another daughter to help with the housework and myriad tasks that kept Leah busy from before sunrise to long after sunset.

After finishing his prayers, Isaac crept down the steps, not willing to wake the noisy brood, hoping for a few moments alone with his wife. Coming up behind her, he cradled his arms around her stomach, playfully pinching the rolls of fat she had developed over the years, even though he knew she was sensitive about the added weight.

Leah slapped his hand away. "Stop that, or I'll give you a good burn with this spoon," she said with a laugh, pointing to the utensil that stirred the barley. "You don't have to worry about a maiden's figure—you're not the one having all these babies!"

"Thank the Almighty for that," he said, remembering with a shiver the birth that had lasted for days. He'd thought he would lose her that time, but she had bounced back with celerity. She'd become a little plumper after each pregnancy, until she resembled the small, round quails sold at the Temple marketplace.

Not that Isaac minded. Leah was beautiful to him, his love, his bride. They presented quite a contrast when they were out together. Isaac had always been tall and thin, almost ascetic-looking, even though he "ate like a starved mule," as Leah always said. His pale skin and soft palms were the telltale signs of a man who worked with his brains for a living, not his hands.

"And so," Leah continued. "What is the schedule for today? How many *hocrim* will you be teaching?"

Isaac inhabited a shadowy world of priests, scribes, and teachers of the Law—all bound by a strict hierarchy, but one that mixed and overlapped in the day's duties. Not learned enough to be a rabbi, though far more educated than many of his boyhood friends, Isaac worked as a scribe, a teacher, and whatever else he was needed for at the Temple in Jerusalem. He spent most of his daylight hours in the Temple, transcribing the holy books, penning letters for those who could not read or write, and participating in discussions with the learned men who sat at the Temple, debating the great issues of the day.

He was paid a small salary for this work, but most of his living came from the later afternoons, when the boys were released from school. Those who showed promise in the villages surrounding Jerusalem would come to the Temple for advanced classes in interpreting Scripture, reading, writing, and mathematics. Only the brightest and best would be allowed to continue in this strictly formatted schooling, and even then, not many families could afford it. It was not unheard of for a particularly bright boy to have his parents, aunts, uncles, and grandparents all helping pay his tuition.

The girls, of course, were lucky to go to school until their twelfth birthdays. Usually, they were brought home at nine or ten to learn the ways of the household. And then, why not? Their place would be having children and raising them, cooking meals, patching clothing, and overseeing the smooth running of the home.

Although Isaac knew in his head that girls did not need the education privileged boys received, the thought of his bright little Leila walking away from the world of scrolls and knowledge filled him with a dull sickness. He had long ago made up his mind to tutor her covertly at home, to improve her writing, to teach her to cipher and read the ancient texts. Leah neither approved nor disapproved, as long as the work around the house was finished. Though she had very little education herself, Leah was proud of her husband's strong bond with his daughter, a bond many Jewish men made little of. A girl, after all, would marry and move away into a new family, caring for her in-laws. It was boys who were prized and valued.

Isaac kissed his wife goodbye and slowly walked the mile to the Temple, his mind lost in thought. His penchant for daydreaming had been his undoing many times, causing him to step in piles of donkey dung or trip off the edge of an uneven road, twisting his ankle. But it was the price Isaac would pay to have some time to himself—time away from his children, his wife, the duties that called at the Temple, and the frenzy of preparations for the Passover. Time to contemplate his place in the world, the state of his people, the work he was called to do.

Would he be able to support another child? His oldest son would soon be ready to apprentice out to Eliazer, the tanner. That would bring in extra money, but not for long. Once a boy became an apprentice, he soon began casting about for a wife, and then all his wages would go to preparing for that future. Perhaps Isaac could pick up extra teaching work, private tutorials for some of the wealthier families. He would quietly put out the word through his Temple contacts.

It pained Isaac that none of his sons showed the promise of rising above the synagogue school and getting extra training to move up in the world. To become a teacher, a scribe—or even a rabbi! But all his sons had followed in Leah's family's footsteps—big, solid young men who took little interest in reading or writing; boys who wanted to be outdoors and working with their hands. Not, of course, that that was a bad thing. But Isaac had hoped for one son who would not only follow in his footsteps, but rise above them to power of his own.

He knew the subject of schooling was a sore one with his sister and her family. They had hoped beyond hope Isaac would recommend their Elkanah for a place in the advanced school, but Isaac could not do that in good conscience. Though his nephew possessed the demeanor for advanced schooling— he was disciplined and preferred to work indoors—he was, well, dull. If Isaac had pushed the matter and gotten the boy accepted, his own reputation would have suffered. Elkanah simply didn't possess the lightning-quick mind that was needed to study Scripture, to argue it with the elders in the Temple, to teach it to young minds. And as for his younger nephew, Bashel ... Isaac just shook his head sadly. He knew his sister and Joachim, her donkey-trading oaf of a husband, were hoping he would measure up, but the boy was a trou- blemaker from the word go. Just last week Isaac had heard rumors of his setting a donkey's tail on fire and sending it careening through the streets of Bethphage. No, he wouldn't do at all.

And he had to laugh at the family's plans to wed Elkanah to his other sister's daughter, Ruchel. What a dream that was! The girl was sassy and well-spoken and had taken care of herself for more than a year in Caiaphas' household. She would run circles around a boy as downtrodden as Elkanah. No, better she found a husband more worthy of her in her master's household. Pairing Ruchel with Elkanah would be like harnessing together a spirited mare and that poor little black donkey Elkanah doted on so much.

But with Leah pregnant again, perhaps Yahweh would favor him with a studious son, one who would sit at the elders' feet at the Temple and drink in their knowledge, like the sponges from the Red Sea they used to soak up spills on the kitchen table.

Isaac could never picture this dream son without letting his mind wander back to the day more than twenty years ago when that strange, learned boy had wandered into the Temple. Isaac had been very young, not much more than eighteen, and assigned some of the lowliest tasks—beating dust from the rug the priests stood on when reading from the Torah, picking wax off the golden candlesticks. A cleaning woman's work, he'd concluded.

Then one day during Passover, he'd found himself on his hands and knees among the seats of the Temple, looking for a golden ring one of the wealthy worshippers had lost.

"It wouldn't kill him to let us find it and put it in the alms box," the old priest had said. "But no, he acts as though he were poverty-stricken." Disgusted, he'd left Isaac alone to search for the ring.

The week had been exhausting. Worshippers from all over the known world had converged on Jerusalem, as they did every year at that time, filling the Temple with almost constant services. The cloying smell of incense clogged Isaac's nostrils, hanging on his clothing long after he returned home at night. Everyone was tired, on edge from having worked many long hours to keep the Temple open to the crowds. The last thing Isaac needed was to crawl around on the stone floor, looking for a piece of jewelry.

"Did you lose something, or is that a new way to pray?"

Isaac looked up quickly, trying to locate the voice, bumping his head on the bench above him. He saw a boy, probably eleven or twelve, watching him intently. He had dark brown hair, the color of walnut skins, and strange, smooth, cinnamon-colored skin. But it was his eyes—not green, not brown—that commanded attention. They were large and curious and filled with mirth.

"I'm praying I might find a ring," Isaac replied, laughing. "One of the men who was here this morning lost it and refuses to leave Jerusalem until it's found." Isaac rubbed the top of his head and fingered the sore spot.

"Well, then, I might as well help you," the boy said, pulling his tunic to his knees and kneeling two rows over. "Where was the man sitting?"

Isaac snorted with disgust. "That's a good question. The first time he was in here, he said he was sitting over there."

Isaac pointed twelve feet away. "Then an hour ago he thought he was sitting right here … so who knows?"

Isaac and the boy continued their crawling—lumbering, really—along the cool stone floor for another fifteen minutes. Suddenly, the boy stopped, stared intently at the seat next to him, and plucked a gold ring from the crack where the flaxen padding of the seat met the back of the bench. "Here it is!" he cried, holding the ring above his head. "It wasn't on the floor at all!"

Isaac heaved a sigh of relief and walked to the boy, tousling his hair and accepting the ring. "You have sharp eyes, my boy," he said. "Almost as sharp as the eagle when it's searching for prey."

"'The eyes of the Lord are everywhere, keeping watch on the wicked and the good,'" the boy murmured, almost to himself, then caught Isaac looking at him. "King Solomon wrote that, you know."

"Yes, I know," Isaac said in wonder. At the time, his own limited experience working with boys of this age was that Scripture almost had to be beaten into them. They would memorize it with rote determination and recite chapters at a time, but they had such difficulty applying a verse or passage to their lives. Suddenly, Isaac realized this boy had been in the Temple with him for the better part of half an hour and did not seem in any hurry to move on.

"What is your name, son?" Isaac asked as he returned to the front of the Temple to check the incense levels. The boy trotted eagerly beside him.

"My name is Yeshua ben Joseph, but my friends call me Yeshi," he said.

"And where are your parents, Yeshi? Do they know you're here?"

The youngster stopped. "Probably not. In fact, by now I'm sure they're starting to worry."

"Well, it's only been half an hour. Why don't you go catch up with them?"

The boy was still for so long Isaac wondered if he was having some kind of fit. Finally, he spoke slowly. "It hasn't been just thirty minutes," he said. "It's been three days since I've seen them."

Isaac grabbed the boy by the elbow and sat him down on the step by the raised platform that held the podium where the Torah was read. "What do you mean? Where do you live?"

Yeshua looked down at his feet, anxiously shuffling them back and forth. "We live in Nazareth, and we were supposed to return after the Passover three days ago, but as we were preparing our cargo, I slipped away to come back to the Temple just once more—oh, it is so beautiful here—and I wanted to talk with the teachers just one more time—and to watch the people bringing sacrifices ... "

Isaac stared at him, not comprehending. "You mean you've been away from your parents for *three days*?" he said incredulously. "Where have you been sleeping? What have you been eating? Haven't you been afraid?"

The laughter that filled the boy's eyes reached his mouth, and he bent forward, giggling, holding his stomach, such a boy despite his brave adventure. "The weather is beautiful, and I've been sleeping in the barn across the Temple courtyard. And the fruit seller down the street has given me all the bruised fruit to eat, and ... "

He trailed off shyly.

"And what?"

"And when I needed to use the pot, I went behind the smithy's forge, in the metal heap." Yeshua seemed proud of his survival skills.

This is incredible, Isaac thought. Somewhere, this boy's parents were frantically looking for him. Evidently, they'd assumed he'd been traveling with another family member, or they would have found him by now. When had they realized he wasn't with any of them?

"And what have you been doing this entire time?" Isaac asked, wondering why he hadn't seen this boy over the past three days. But then, in the crush of worshippers, it would have been easy to overlook a young child.

"Talking with the teachers whenever I could," Yeshua replied, a rapturous look engulfing his face. "Oh, sir ... "

"It's Isaac."

"Oh, Isaac, we discussed Isaiah and the prophecies he foretold of the coming of the Messiah, and then how Micah, too, had recounted those prophecies, as had Zephaniah, and I asked them about what Isaiah meant when he said, 'I saw the Lord, high and exalted, seated on a throne; and the train of his robe filled the temple.'"

Isaac sat with his mouth open. Either this boy, this Yeshi, was mentally touched, or he had one of the greatest minds of any child his age. Isaac continued to sit as Yeshua regaled him with tales of his conversations with the teachers, as well as stories of living rough in Jerusalem, including how he'd managed to convince a pretty girl at the well to draw him a drink that morning.

It was one of the most unusual interludes in Isaac's life. When he went home that evening to Leah, his new bride, he recounted everything that had happened, along with the crazed anxiety of Yeshua's parents when they'd finally returned to the Temple several hours later. The boy had seemed unfazed, even though he surely deserved a whipping for slipping off like that.

But Yeshua had calmly kissed his mother on the cheek and said, "Mother, Mother, why were you searching for me? Didn't you know I had to be in my Father's house?" Everyone standing nearby had stood, transfixed, as the boy slipped his arm through his mother's and led her and his father out of the Temple.

At the last minute, as they were about to descend the steps, the boy had turned and run back to Isaac. "It was nice meeting you, Isaac," he'd said, puffing slightly. "I'm glad we found that ring."

Isaac had run his hand through Yeshua's dark-brown curls and hugged him closely. "Don't scare your mother that way again," he'd said, laughing. "You've about given her a heart attack."

Then Yeshi had raised his hand to wave, turned, and ran back to his parents.

That evening, Leah had agreed the whole affair was quite strange and promptly forgotten about it.

But Isaac had never let the memory of that boy—Yeshua— leave his heart. He often wondered what had happened to him. He was certainly meant for extraordinary things.

Perhaps he would have a son like him.

Little did Isaac know he would meet this strange boy— now a man—that very day, in an encounter as bizarre as the first. But then again, peculiar things often happened in the Temple the week of Passover.

- LILITH -

Lilith ducked into the doorway of the courtyard, hiding in the shadows from the masses sitting, dancing, talking, and drinking at the wedding feast. Her head pounded, and the shrill notes of the flute weren't helping. She needed a few moments to herself to breathe and rub away the pains in her temples.

It had been a *disaster*—all of it. Despite months of planning and making lists and hiring extra help and threatening vendors, the wedding had been a debacle from the beginning. At first it was small things, ones only the women would notice. The men—louts that they were—would only complain if there wasn't enough food and drink. They wouldn't see those minuscule details their wives, mothers, and sisters would talk about for months to come at the well.

Ezra and Shoshannah were expected at the feast around sundown, though everyone knew that time could vary. Shoshannah's home was only a few miles away, and as the young men and maidens went to wait for the bride and groom to celebrate with them on the road, the older folks waited in Lilith's courtyard. Her husband's sister-in-law had helped prepare the last-minute details, and the servants had hurriedly put the final touches in place.

But as the hours dragged on—first one, then two, then finally three hours after sunset—everyone slowly realized there must be a problem. Was Ezra too drunk to make the trip? Had Shoshannah's father thrown up a roadblock at the last minute? Everyone remembered the wedding of Hadod's daughter the year before, how Hadod had screamed curses from the upstairs window when his daughter's groom had come to collect her, trying to foil the ceremony and shaming himself in the process. But surely that wasn't the case here? Just two weeks before, Naahum and Lilith had invited Shoshannah's parents for a meal, and they'd been jollity itself, never alluding to any problems with the impending nuptials.

Finally, the first faint strains of the wedding party could be heard coming down the road. The young people were clanging whatever instruments or homemade noisemakers they could find to tell everyone along the route the bride and her bridegroom were coming. While a few of the party had flutes or small cymbals, many banged together bricks, or sheets of tin, or simply sang at the top of their lungs. Those seated in the courtyard could tell the chaos was half-hearted, that the gaiety was forced. A knot formed in Lilith's stomach as she tried to imagine what was wrong.

Finally, the clutch of young girls who attended the bride made their way into the courtyard. Lilith glimpsed her niece,

Adaliah, with the throng. Edging her way through the group, Lilith grabbed Adaliah's elbow and herded her to the relative privacy of a hyssop bush.

"Where has everyone been?" she hissed, glancing sideways to make sure they were not overheard. "The bride and groom were expected hours ago!"

Adaliah looked tired, and Lilith noticed her eyes were red. The girl avoided her aunt's gaze and mumbled, "Shoshannah was not yet ready to go."

Lilith dropped her niece's elbow and stood back in amazement. "What do you mean? That is absurd! Shoshannah and her family have known the date of this ceremony for almost a year! Her parents could send anything she didn't have packed later!"

Adaliah looked her aunt square in the eyes, and the older woman noticed the pain and sorrow there. "Please, Aunt, do not ask any questions. The bride and groom are arriving." She made a movement to head toward the festivities, but Lilith would not be put off so easily.

"You—will—tell—me—what—is—going—on. Right this minute," she spit, suddenly worried for her son. "Tell me *right now*, or I'll go and ask Ezra himself."

With a panicked gesture, Adaliah pulled her aunt even deeper into the bush's shadows. "It's nothing, really," she assured her with false sweetness. "Shoshannah is young, and when Ezra and his friends showed up and began calling for her under her windows, she ... well, she had a young bride's change of heart and wasn't sure if she wanted to go."

"But to keep everyone waiting for *hours*?" Lilith countered. "Of course, a girl is nervous ... "

She trailed off, remembering her own fear and trepidation at making that journey with her new husband. "But what happened? Did she refuse to come?"

Again, Adaliah was evasive. "She's here now, and so is Ezra. Let us go and join those who are ready to celebrate."

The sick knot in Lilith's stomach grew tighter. Something was very, very wrong. She had known it from the very beginning, when Ezra had approached them and asked Naahum to make a betrothal agreement with a girl they hadn't even known he was seeing. How he had refused to be part of the agreement. And the few times Lilith had seen Shoshannah—at the market, at dinner—she'd always been polite, but distant and preoccupied. Not at all as giddy and excited as a bride should be, never once mentioning the goods she was putting away for her marriage or commenting on the rooms Ezra was adding to their home.

Well, it was too late now. Lilith swiped her hand across her brow, as if pushing away all the worries that consumed her. She had a courtyard full of people, and she had to entertain them in a manner befitting the family of a well-to-do wool merchant. She would *not* shame her son or his new bride.

And so she had joined the rest of the crowd, noting her son's glazed look—too much wine? Or was he still nursing a broken heart? She took in her new daughter-in-law's wan complexion—was she simply washed out by the pale blue dress she wore? Or did she have secrets too deep to share? What, exactly, had happened earlier that evening?

The toasts had gone on, and the Cyprian wine flowed. More neighbors and friends stopped by. For one pure moment of unadulterated joy, Mary found her and the two women embraced.

"Oh, Mary, it has been so long," Lilith wept tears of joy. "We must not let the few miles between our villages keep us from seeing each other."

Mary grabbed Lilith's hand and squeezed it fervently. "It is so good to see you and celebrate your son's wedding." Her large, liquid umber eyes danced in the firelight. "Yeshua and his friends will be coming later this evening. I only wish Joseph were here … "

Her voice trailed off, and her face shuttered as she was lost in memories. Then, with a small shake of her head, Mary cast off her sadness and turned again to Lilith.

"What preparations you must have made to host your son's wedding feast!" she said in admiration. "I've given up on Yeshua ever marrying; he spent so many years caring for me after Joseph's death, and now, well, he and his friends … "

A worm of distaste wriggled into Lilith's brain, but she would not worry Mary with it. "It will be good to see Yeshua again, and his friends are more than welcome here," she said hospitably as she and Mary joined the others, dancing with the women and listening with laughter and shouts of agreement as the toasts continued—one from Naahum, then more from Shoshannah's father and brothers.

Several hours later, the first signs of trouble in the meal preparations had reached Lilith's ears. A young servant, hired for the occasion from the nearby village, had sidled up to her, bowing and cringing as if he feared her wrath. Well, Lilith had been overwrought the last several weeks, and maybe she'd taken it out on the servants...most of them with brains the size of peas.

"Well?" she asked impatiently. "What is needed?"

The young man—no more than twelve or thirteen, she realized—spoke so softly he could hardly be heard above the droning of the reed instruments. "My lord, the master of the servants, has asked me to tell you the Samarian wine will soon run out."

Lilith looked at him, stunned. That could not be! The Cyprian wine should have lasted at least two hours, then the Samarian wine at least six more. She did a quick reckoning on her fingers. The guests would stay the night, celebrating, then spend the next day sleeping off the festivities. At sundown the following evening, they would rise and start the whole thing over. This could go on for several days, with the staunchest partygoers staying six or seven nights. Tomorrow, she would send a servant to the market to buy more wine, but there was nowhere she could get more at this hour. If the Samarian wine was almost out, that meant they had run through everything—*everything* they had. They would be out of wine before midnight, which would shame Naahum and his family. It would be said at the well tomorrow that Naahum was tighter than a new wineskin with his *shekels*.

That he refused to have enough wine at the feast to encourage the guests to leave. That Naahum had not provided enough wine because he did not approve of the marriage.

Obviously, old Jeremiah's flea-brained son had bungled the order, taking the money they had paid and not delivering enough wine. *I will see him at the gate in front of the elders,* she vowed, her anger beginning to pound in her head. But for now, there were practical necessities to see to. She looked at the young boy and told him to deliver a message to the master of the servants.

"We must water down the Samarian wine immediately." Then she prayed that by the time the guests had run through the red, treacly wine they wouldn't realize they were out.

But still the guests had poured in. Distant relatives Lilith had not planned on attending, old neighbors they had not seen in years, people she didn't know at all and assumed were part of Shoshannah's family. Now in the doorway of the courtyard, she massaged her temples, knowing that any way she looked at the situation, it was a disaster. All she wanted to do was crawl into the cool darkness of her bedchamber and draw the tapestries.

Mary saw Lilith standing apart from the festivities and threaded her way through the throng to take her hand. "Come, Lilith, it's a time to be joyful," she said, urging her back to the fire before noticing the drawn lines of pain on the younger woman's face.

"Are you sick?" Mary asked, dropping her hand and putting an arm around Lilith's shoulders.

"Sick at heart," Lilith said with a wry laugh. "The servants told me over an hour ago that the wine is running out. That idiot of a wine seller obviously didn't bring the full order, though he was paid well to do so. I ordered what was left to be watered down, but even that must be getting to the end." She looked down in shame, and when Mary said nothing, she lifted her face and looked at her dear friend and cousin. "Oh, Mary, this wedding feast *must* go well. So many things have not been right about this betrothal ... "

"Yes, yes, I know." Mary's hand stroked Lilith's feverish forehead. Lilith wondered what she'd heard about the strange situation, about the reluctant bride, the bridegroom with clay feet, the inadequate refreshments. Mary took Lilith's elbow and led her to a nearby stool.

"Here, you have a seat and I'll get a cup of *watered* wine," she said with a chuckle. Even Lilith could not resist a sick giggle. "I'll go and see what I can do."

Lilith shook her head. "What do you mean, 'what you can do?'" Lilith asked with resignation. "The market is closed. We'll simply have to run out and look like fools."

"Maybe not," Mary said enigmatically. "Just rest for a while."

- DEBORAH -

Even a year later, it was hard to believe any of it had happened. When Deborah dwelled on the events of the past twelve months, it was as if she recalled them through the mists of a dream—one that began so pleasantly, then so rapidly turned into a nightmare.

Of course, it had all started with Seneca. Deborah could still hardly whisper his name without her insides fluttering. She'd loved him more than she'd loved any other man, even though she'd known from the beginning it was a doomed relationship. Even so, she'd carried on, could not have turned from it even if she'd had a sword at her throat.

Seneca. His broad shoulders so wide in his soldier's uniform, his neck, face, and forearms burned an umber brown. Deborah would tease him that he looked like the farmers in the hills who harvested grapes and olives and brought them to her small village just outside Jerusalem to sell on the sixth day of each week. After setting up their stalls, they would strip their tunics off behind the buildings of the market square and wash up before beginning the day's selling. And Deborah, who often traveled that street on her way to work in the herb seller's stall, would avert her eyes from their pale, white bodies and red necks and forearms.

Seneca. So handsome with his aquiline nose and dark blue eyes, his shaggy brown hair that grew so fast. Just thinking of him even all these months later still brought a stab of pain to her heart. It could never be. She was an observant Jew, and he was a Roman soldier.

It was crazy how things had gotten so far out of control. Deborah was a mason's daughter—a pretty, polite girl, but no great beauty, as her mother often reminded her. Deborah had married her cousin, Aaron, when she was fourteen and thought she had a good life ahead of her.

Aaron was apprenticed to her father as a young boy just out of synagogue school, and Deborah knew at an early age that he favored her. She'd find him hanging around her house in the mornings, long after he should have been off to the mason's shop, offering to lift heavy baskets and haul water for her from the well. Deborah had taken advantage of his generosity only once, when she allowed him to walk with her and haul the heavy clay flagons that usually rested gracefully on the hips and heads of the village women. Hauling water was women's work, and the teasing had been unmerciful. She'd never allowed it again.

Working with her father, Aaron learned masonry quickly and surpassed his teacher in talent and aptitude. It wasn't long before Aaron was being called out to jobs in outlying villages, or working on the local synagogue and even doing stonework for the Roman authorities in Jerusalem.

Everyone told her what a blessed woman she was—with a husband working for the Romans! Yes, they were feared as they marched through the streets in their awesome displays of power, but they mostly left the Jews alone … as long as the people of Israel kept to their place, worshipped Hashem quietly, and didn't try to upset the status quo. Everyone knew what happened to zealots who overturned the olive basket, so to speak, by preaching against the Roman government. So futile.

"It's like an ant spitting on a giant," her father used to say. "We might as well live and let live until the Messiah comes to rescue us."

Working for the Romans offered more than just prestige. The money they threw around for even the most menial jobs was extravagant, though Aaron had always felt guilty taking it, knowing most of it had come from his own people's taxes. The Romans and their cronies—Jews who had turned traitor and were willing to betray their own people to please their overlords—were always waiting, looking for an opportunity to tax one more thing. They sat at the city gates, these wheedling little snakes, always sizing up the produce brought to market, always rifling through the baskets of fine woven linen the women of Capernaum embroidered with such pride and joy. Always looking for a way to squeeze one more *denarius* out of people who barely eked out a living. They were detested, and Aaron could not help but compare himself to them, even though he worked hard and made his living honestly.

Only one thing had marred the joy Deborah felt in her marriage: There had been no child. Every month, Deborah had prayed the season of blood would not take her, that the joy she and Aaron felt together in their marriage bed would result in a child.

A boy, oh dear Yahweh, send me a boy, she would implore, imagining Aaron's face as she presented him with an heir. *Oh, dear Redeemer, even barren Hannah of the ancient times was given a child, as were Rachel and Sarah. Look on your handmaiden and send me a child, I pray.*

But every time the moon turned dark, her blood would flow and her days of seclusion would begin, as prescribed by the Law of Moses. She would stay at home, defiled, unable to touch her husband or even prepare his food. Aaron would avoid her during these times, eating his meals at the home of his widowed mother and sleeping on a mat next to the fire in the kitchen.

Eventually, Deborah even kept away from the well. It was impossible not to draw water every day, but instead of going first thing each morning, as the women of the village did—gossiping, washing each other's hair, comparing recipes—Deborah began going in the cool of the evening. That way, she'd only encounter travelers looking for a place to stay or the odd merchant who needed more water to clean his stall.

If she didn't stay away, her heart would break. Her mother and sisters were too sharp-eyed, as well as sharp-tongued, to keep their mouths shut when they met her at the well, reaching down into its mouth to pull up the wooden-slatted bucket overflowing with the life-giving wetness that was so scarce in their country.

Every month they would ask, "Well? Has El Elyon stirred your womb? Are you blessed among women?"

It became an ache in Deborah's heart to see them, to evade their questions and their supposedly helpful advice—eat a mandrake freshly pulled from the soil; go see Widow ben Ananin, who lived outside the city wall and had a purse of unusual herbs said to aid fertility; have relations with Aaron in this position, or that position. It was embarrassing and degrading, and Deborah had refused to put up with it any longer.

Four years passed in her marriage, and all of Deborah's childhood friends became mothers, some with quite large broods. Why, even Abrah, the ugly, squat girl who had grown up three streets over—even she had been blessed by the Most High with two strong, healthy sons. Why had the Lord chosen to close her womb?

Then one evening—as she was hurrying home from the well with water for the next day's washing—her life changed forever. She knew it was getting late and that Aaron would be home soon, wanting his dinner. Some of the precious water sloshed over the side of her pot as she stumbled on a crack in the dusty roadway.

As she entered the small barnyard outside their home, Deborah was amazed to see her father and younger brother standing there, her father with his arms sternly folded across his chest. Deborah instantly knew something of great importance had happened—she never saw her family at this time of day, when they would be gathering around their own table. And then there was the look on her father's face. His usually merry eyes were sorrowful and lifeless. His large mouth—usually wide with laughter that showed off his perfectly even, white teeth—was tightly compressed. Her brother stood with his arms at his sides, as if his hands had grown too big for his body and he didn't know where to put them.

Deborah strode forward to meet them, setting her pot down carefully so as not to spill any more water.

"Father," she said, her hands outstretched, "what a blessing to see you. Why are you here at this time of day? Is something wrong with Mother?"

Her father clutched her hands. "Deborah," he began and faltered. "Deborah … it's Aaron."

As a child, Deborah had been kicked in the stomach by a colt when she'd foolishly wandered behind him. The sharp imprint of his hoof on her mid-section had plagued her for weeks. In that moment, the same sense of recoil hit her, and she would have fallen to her knees if her father hadn't clutched her hands so tightly. She could not speak.

"Deborah, let's go inside," her father said gently, but Deborah made no move to pull herself from being a crumpled heap on her father's shoulder. Quietly, he picked her up, carried her across the threshold of the little house, and laid her on the low couch that sat next to the fire. Gently, as if speaking to a small child, he told her in staccato sentences the little there was to know. How Aaron had been working at the watchtower for the Roman guard, which Deborah already knew. It was a large job, one that would take two men several months to complete. Aaron had taken on an apprentice of his own—a thirteen-year-old boy—to finish. Deborah had even gone with Aaron once to marvel at the huge stones that would be added to the already towering structure.

"He was below, setting the mortar on the base," her father began. "The boy was up above. Aaron was counting the stones on the parapets, getting them ready to work on tomorrow." Her father looked into Deborah's vacant, glazed eyes and wondered if she was taking any of this in. "One of the stones on the parapet tipped over the side and fell on Aaron. It was instant, Deborah—he didn't suffer."

Deborah didn't remember anything after that. In fact, the next few weeks seemed shrouded in a thick woolen blanket, the kind her grandmother had woven when she was still living. Her father and Aaron's father took care of all the burial details—sitting *shiva* for ten days with ten men to mourn Aaron; lining up the professional mourners, who made such a racket and seemed so false that Deborah finally told them to leave; and making arrangements for the burial spices that would be placed in the strips of cloth that wrapped the body.

Deborah didn't help with any of it. Her parents would not let her see his body, as Aaron's head had been badly crushed, and they wanted to spare her that. They spoon-fed her lamb broth. They tucked her in, as they would a baby. They took her by the hand and led her where she needed to go, then left her alone the rest of the time. Well, not *really* alone. No one let her out of their sight for more than a few moments. Deborah heard her parents whispering, trying to decide how to approach the subject of her moving back home with them.

Deborah pretended not to hear. This was her home, unusual as the circumstances had been. It was almost a given that a young married couple would move into an extra room or build an addition to the groom's parents' house. They were almost never allowed the privacy of a separate house, but Aaron had done well for himself and been able to purchase the small plot of land. Then he'd built this house with his own hands. It was hers in spirit, even if legally only Aaron's name was on the deed. Deborah could never move back in with her mother and younger sisters, not after having a home of her own, a kitchen of her own, ways of making her own bread and stew, the freedom to go to the well when she wished.

But as she soon discovered, a woman's worth in Judea was tied to her husband—something Deborah no longer had. She was one step above being property, a thing to be passed back and forth, like a pot or a linen tunic. Thus, several weeks after Aaron's death, her father sat down with her, slapping both hands against his knees. Deborah knew the reckoning had come.

"Well, Debree," he said, reverting to a childish nickname. Instantly, Deborah realized she was no longer a grown woman in his eyes, but a child. "It's best that you move back with your mother and me. You know you have a place there as long as you need it."

"I don't need a place, Father," Deborah replied, turning her head away to look at the wall. "I have a home and I'm perfectly fine staying here."

"But there's a problem with that." Her father paused. "Aaron's younger brother, Jeshreel, is marrying in a couple months, and they need a place to live …"

He trailed off, letting the news soak in. Seeing Deborah's distraught face, he decided to take command and end this misery quickly.

"This was your home while Aaron was living. But with no father, on his death, the deed reverts to his oldest brother. You have no choice now, Deborah," he said firmly. "After the Sabbath, your mother and sisters will come and help you pack everything, and you'll move back home." Seeing the tears welling up in Deborah's eyes, her father softened. "Daughter, things will go well, you'll see. And you are young, and certainly after the time of mourning is over, there will be other men—I know that Nahor's son has been dropping hints …"

Deborah looked at him, incredulous. Then she laughed bitterly. "My husband has been dead for less than three weeks, and already you're marrying me off, Father?"

Ashamed, her father dropped his eyes and left, closing the door softly behind him.

Three days later, for the first time since Aaron's death, Deborah found herself truly alone in the house. She knew she needed to make lists of what to take back to her parents' home and what to leave. Aaron's brother had been very kind, settling a large sum of money on her, which he hadn't needed to do. But now Deborah was out of place, and her presence was awkward for Aaron's family. They wanted— and needed—to move on. Deborah wanted nothing more than for everything to be as it had been ... and if that wasn't possible, to stay exactly where she was.

A loud knock at the front door startled her from her reverie. *Probably another neighbor.* They had come for weeks following Aaron's death, some to bring mounds of food she could never eat, some to hold her in their arms and mourn with her, others to simply see Deborah's misery firsthand and catch snippets of private conversation that could be spread throughout the village. Deborah did not have the strength to deal with it that day. Wearily, she went to the door, already framing excuses for why she couldn't visit.

The sun blazed behind him, silhouetting his large body in the doorway. Even though Deborah could not see his face, she could tell instantly from his dress that he was a

Roman soldier. A spear of terror paralyzed her. She could say nothing, do nothing, move not a muscle.

"I am searching for the widow of Aaron the Mason," the man said in broken Aramaic, obviously struggling with the language. "I have ... "

He floundered for the words, then gave up, pulling a small bag of coins out of the sack thrown over his soldier. "These are—for you."

Deborah didn't know what to make of this strange scene—a Roman soldier appearing on her doorstep, speaking Aramaic to her, producing a bag of money. She simply stared at him, not sure how to respond.

"May I come in?" He gestured into the room behind her, and Deborah mutely stepped aside, even though her mind screamed so many things. *He is a Gentile. He is a Roman soldier. He is a man and I am now an unmarried woman. I have no chaperone here. He is everything I should avoid.* Though her mind registered these things, she felt helpless as she stood clutching the door. Soon only one thought remained.

He is a Roman soldier. I must obey him.

He stepped into the room, out of the sun, and she could now see he was carrying a helmet under one arm and that his hair was the color of the dark brown cattails she had harvested from the nearby lake and turned into a dye for Aaron's tunics. And it was long, shaggy. Deborah had never seen a soldier with such long hair, though when she thought about it, she had seen very few soldiers without their helmets. Perhaps they all marched with heads like lion manes.

Everything about the soldier was strange to her. He was taller than Jewish men and his shoulders were broader. He was clean-shaven, whereas the men she knew grew beards in adulthood. His eyes—oh, his eyes were so different than what she was used to—a piercing blue, the color of the stream that ran outside the village when the sun struck it. She stood dumbly, realizing she had yet to say a single word, had offered no hospitality.

"Please, have a seat," she said, bustling over with a stool from beside the fireplace. She vaguely waved her hand behind her. "I've been cleaning, I'm getting ready to move, my parents … "

"I understand," he said hesitantly, trying out the words of her people. He seated himself gingerly on the stool, which was too close to the floor for his height. "My sympathies to you on your loss. I bring the … " he fumbled for the right word. "The payment for your husband's work on the watchtower."

As he laid the bag on the table, Deborah said nothing but wondered why a Roman soldier would visit her home. Why hadn't they simply sent a courier or a messenger boy? As if reading her mind, the man went on.

"There is too much money here—that's why I bring it," he said simply, then paused. "My name is Seneca." And when the next pause grew awkward, he added, "And I don't know Aramaic very well."

Deborah burst into laughter and Seneca joined her. It broke the tension, and they conversed haltingly—he unsure of the correct words, she unsure of whether she should be talking to him at all. But it was so easy to converse with him, and she realized she was lonely to the core. Her family had been kind, Aaron's family had been tolerant, but she was the spotted sheep now, without a real place until her father could tidy things up by marrying her off again. She missed talking with Aaron, talking about male things. She missed sharing his daily problems on the worksite and telling him about the fight two village women had had at the well that day. She missed the small talk at meals and as she was mixing the bread. She missed *companionship*.

And so she learned Seneca was stationed in Judea—for several years, most likely—and that he longed for his family and his home on a villa outside Rome. His was a poor farm family, and they had followed the custom of having the second son take up military life. After all, he pointed out, there would be little for him in the way of inheritance—his older brother would claim that.

"The countryside is very beautiful," he said, his eyes drifting off as if he were seeing it again. "When the sun sets behind the hills, the sky turns purple and the air is cool. Our family sits down to eat, and it is a joyous time."

Deborah couldn't fathom that people who lived so far from her village did the same ordinary things she did—and had done—with Aaron. It seemed unreal that Seneca could be homesick for a place Deborah would never see, for people she would never know. Her life had been so circumscribed here in the village that she seldom thought much beyond what she was going to cook for meals tomorrow or how best to get a blood stain out of Aaron's linen undershirt.

Suddenly, as if remembering other things he was supposed to be doing, Seneca got to his feet and picked up his helmet from on the table.

"I must go," he said with a military precision that so jarred Deborah she thought she'd imagined their previous conversation. He stepped to the door and turned around. "I hope this has not made trouble for you … me in your home … I know it's not allowed … "

For the first time since Aaron's death, Deborah felt in control of something. She raised her chin and stood up straighter.

"There is no trouble," she said resolutely. "There will be *no* trouble."

Later, she would think back on those words—on her naïveté—and laugh.

- SHOSHANNAH -

Shoshannah plied her fine bone needle through the ecru wool tunic, which slipped easily through her fingers. It was beautiful material, lightweight and high quality, procured by her father-in-law from a group of Syrian traders. Ezra had carried the bolt home on his shoulders one evening, offering it to Shoshannah with an awkward gesture.

"My father thought you would like this," he'd said shyly. "Since you are such a good seamstress ... "

She had eagerly reached for the material, giving Ezra a warm smile.

In the four months since the wedding, the couple's life had been quiet, but not unpleasant. They had each come into the marriage acknowledging the other had hurts better left unspoken, at least for now. Ezra had allowed Shoshannah privacy, while also bringing small gifts to her from the marketplace, or that he'd found on his way home from the fields or working with his father. She might be surprised with a bouquet of wildflowers or a piece of ribbon the color of the Palestinian sky. Ezra's taciturn thoughtfulness touched her.

And Shoshannah had put his latest gift to good use. After making herself a shawl for the chill Galilean nights, she had enough left to make two tunics, a sort of undergarment for men. In the heat of the day, a tunic could be worn alone or with a shirt beneath it. In the chillier winter months and the evenings, most men would throw a cape or blanket shawl around their shoulders over their tunics.

But the tunics Shoshannah made from this wool would be for special occasions, not for the dirt and sweat of a workday. They would be exquisite, complete with a row of decorative embroidery at the bottom, hallmarks of her renowned needlework. Her husband would wear his with pride.

When she had finished Ezra's tunic, Shoshannah had cast about for someone to give the second tunic to. A scene from the night of her wedding niggled in the back of her mind, of her mother-in-law's cousin, Mary, fussing at her son, Yeshua, near the courtyard wall about the condition of the tunic he was wearing. Shoshannah had gathered it was frayed, with the seams beginning to tear apart.

"Really, son, you can't go out in public like this," Mary had gently remonstrated. "At least let me sew this up before you leave again!"

"I'm sorry, Mother," Yeshua had said with tired patience in his voice. "It's hard to keep things in good repair when we're sleeping in fields and along the road. These seams pull loose all the time."

"What you need," Mary had replied, fingering the stitches, "is a seamless garment—one sewn from a single piece … "

"What you mean is I need something expensive!" Yeshua laughed. "You worry too much about your fully grown son. I'll get along fine."

Shoshannah had grinned to herself at the thought of a mother clucking over a son who was nearing thirty as if he were yet a young boy. But the conversation had given her an idea. She owed Yeshua so much after that evening. Perhaps she could sew something for him, something that would hold up better than the pieced tunic he had been wearing.

As Shoshannah rethreaded her needle and worked on hemming the tunic she would give Yeshua as a gift, she relived the night of her wedding. Well, at least as much of it as she could. So many parts were a blur. There was so much she could not remember … or had chosen not to remember.

She had really thought she was going to rise above it all, as the days of preparation pushed her nearer the appointed date of her wedding. She had been busy, with little time to think about her plight. There were dishes to collect, garments to sew, gifts to prepare for the wedding party, and visits to the rooms Ezra was painstakingly adding to his family's home for the two of them. His pride was evident as he pointed out the fine craftsmanship of the cupboard in the corner, the beams on the ceiling.

On the evening of the celebration—as the sun began to fall and the first stars poked through the cloudy sky—a sense of calm had come over her. She had made her decision—she was marrying a good man, and she would live a life that brought honor to his name.

Half an hour before Ezra and the rest of the bridal party were expected to arrive, she heard her father's angry voice in the courtyard outside her window, followed by Hannah's heavy, thudding steps running up the stairway. Shoshannah's little sister burst into her room with a wild look in her eyes.

"What in the world is going on?" Shoshannah demanded. "Is Father fighting with someone out there?"

Hannah was out of breath and put her hands on her knees before gasping out an answer.

"It's Nathaniel ... he's ... he's out there with Father ... and ... he ... wants to see you."

Their mother barreled into the room after Hannah, her arm reaching for her younger daughter's shoulder, evidently having tried to stop her from getting to Shoshannah.

The mention of Nathaniel's name made Shoshannah's stomach flop, and she immediately felt sick. So many sensations flooded her—shame, panic, anger, longing. She dropped into the chair beside her bed and stared at Hannah with vacant eyes.

"I do not want to see him," she said with a dead voice. She heard her father's shouts as he continued to berate someone in the courtyard. And then she heard it—Nathaniel's voice, his words slow and slurred. He was obviously drunk.

Loudly, and right below her window, she heard him shout. "I am sorry! I was a fool! Shoshannah, talk to me!"

As Shoshannah made a motion to move to the window, her mother grabbed her by the arm. "You will *not* talk to him," she hissed. "You will not see him. You will not change your mind. You will not shame our family … again."

The hard, flinty look on her mother's face hit Shoshannah as if someone had tossed a glass of icy water from the well on her head. She sagged back into the chair and put her hands over her ears. She would not listen. She would not hear.

The rest of the night passed in a dream. She remembered her sisters, her mother, her friends in her room rubbing her head with cool lavender oil as she lay on the bed. She remembered urgent voices telling her she needed to get up and meet her groom, that she needed to parade down the road to the celebration. And all she wanted to do was fall into a deep sleep of forgetfulness.

Eventually, she dragged herself from her bed, into the clamoring throng in her courtyard. Ezra's friends sensed something was wrong, but no one made mention of it. Ezra stepped forward, offering his hand, his face white and drawn. There was no sign of Nathaniel or of her father. She vaguely wondered where they had gone. Had Ezra seen—or even talked—to Nathaniel? Had her father brought him back to his own house? Had he beaten Nathaniel senseless and left him alone in the fields? Or was Nathaniel waiting along the way, planning to make another scene? The possibilities drained Shoshannah of her little remaining strength. She didn't care anymore. She just wanted to the entire celebration to be over.

Once they'd walked the dusty miles to Ezra's home—the tinny notes of celebration sounding so false—the feeble celebrations began. Shoshannah was introduced to dozens of people, mostly Ezra's family. Their faces swirled into one loud mass of laughing, braying partygoers, many of them grabbing her hands, trying to put their hands on her head in blessing, stepping on the hem of her robe. It was awful, awful.

When she heard the whispered rumors that the wine was running out, she laughed out loud. Of course! What else could go wrong that evening? Even though the celebrations were the responsibility of the groom's family, running out of wine would shame her family, too. The gossips at the well would talk for days about how Shoshannah, that prize lily among girls, had married a man too tight to provide for his guests. Perhaps—they would say it in that simpering, knowing way—she wasn't as special as her family had always thought she was. But let it be. She didn't care enough to say anything.

Then Shoshannah overheard that snippet of conversation between Mary and her son, Yeshua, that strange cousin of Ezra's who had showed up at the party with a band of burly men, all of them obviously ill at ease until they got a little wine in them. Then they began dancing animatedly and singing louder than most of the other guests. *Maybe that's where the wine has gone,* she remembered thinking. Those men seemed to have had plenty of it!

She vaguely wondered what would happen when everyone found out the wine had run dry. If Hashem were truly good, the guests would be disillusioned enough to simply go home and leave them in peace! But that did not seem destined to happen.

She noticed a flurry of activity among the servants, then saw Yeshua standing among them, as if he were giving them directions. The first prickle of interest stirred in her as she watched the tableau. One of the servants was shaking his head doubtfully; another watched Yeshua intently, hanging on his every word. In the end, they all dispersed, carrying the huge water jars used for ceremonial washing. Some of the younger servants, boys really, could barely haul the crocks that were as large as their slight bodies. They headed in the direction of the well.

This is very odd, Shoshannah thought. All the ceremonial washing had been done before they'd eaten. There was no call to wash again. She had heard strange things about Ezra's cousin, this Yeshua. Was he going to ask everyone to rewash? Was he some sort of religious zealot, who didn't think the first wash had been thorough enough? What was the point when everyone would probably leave soon, once they found out the wine was running out?

The musicians were well into a song praising Shoshannah's beauty and grace—"The Lily of the Morning," they called it. She sat with a pasted smile on her face, enduring it with the best grace she could muster. A servant girl, the one assigned to wait on the bride and groom, hurried to her side, lugging a clay pitcher, moving so fast wine sloshed over its lip.

"Take it easy, Chavah," she chastised the young girl. "From the sound of things, there isn't much wine to spare."

"No, mistress, you won't believe what's happened." The girl reached for Shoshannah's glass and poured it half full of purply-red liquid. "Taste this … just taste it."

Shoshannah took a hesitant sip, recognizing the wine's quality immediately from the smell alone. This wasn't the vinegar-like brew that often passed for wine in Cana. This was the finest Cyprian wine—thick, rich, sweet, and potent. This wine was better than the cup she'd drunk hours before.

"Interesting." Shoshannah grinned, handing the cup to her new husband. "Evidently they found a few more pitchers of wine hidden somewhere?"

"No, mistress, you don't understand. That man, that Yeshua, he told us to fill the ceremonial jars with water." Chavah paused to turn and fill a cup in the outthrust hand of a guest. "We told him we had already washed, that we didn't need any more water tonight, but he was insistent."

Shoshannah thought about the strange scene she had witnessed earlier. "Go on," she urged, frowning.

"We all thought he was a little crazy, but his mother came over and told us to do what he said." Chavah smirked. "We know how much our mistress thinks of her cousin Mary, so we did it." The servant girl straightened up and started moving to the next set of guests, but Shoshannah grabbed her arm.

"Wait a minute," she said impatiently. "What happened next?"

Chavah looked at Shoshannah as if she were denser than the wool sheared in springtime. "He turned that water into wine! After we filled the jars and brought them to him, he prayed over them and asked for a dipper." Chavah's eyes were large. "I ran to get him a gourd, he dipped it into the jar, tasted it, and smiled. Then he told the rest of us to taste it. It was wine—*expensive* wine!"

Shoshannah looked at her in disbelief. "Chavah, you are old enough not to believe in magic tricks, or sleight of hand, or whatever this Yeshua pulled off." Her tone was dismissive. "Someone traded the water jars for ones filled with wine. He was just playing a joke on all of you."

But Chavah shook her head adamantly. "No, mistress, I was with those jars the entire time. He really turned that water into wine. He is no ordinary man—I know it!"

Voices were calling out, guests wanting their glasses refilled, and Chavah hurried off to do her job. Shoshannah shook her head, unable to accept such an incredible story. She turned to see if Ezra had heard Chavah's tale, but he was engaged in conversation with the big, ruddy-faced man sitting next to him.

"Ezra, I've got to hand it to you!" The man's voice boomed across the entire courtyard. "Most grooms serve the best wine first to get their guests drunk so they won't notice the swill that comes out later, but you're a tricky one! This is the best wine we've had tonight!"

Ezra was giving a weak imitation of a smile, refusing to catch Shoshannah's eye. He was embarrassed, she could see. Maybe he really didn't know about the wine that had been brought out at the last moment. Did he know where it had been hidden? Or did he believe the crazy story the servants were telling?

Reflecting on that night, Shoshannah concluded the whole evening had been very odd: Nathaniel's showing up at the last moment, the sad little parade to her new home, then the debacle of the wine running out. She still wasn't sure what to make of Yeshua and the miraculously appearing Cyprian wine, but she didn't care. He had helped her and Ezra and his family to save face, and for that she was grateful.

Shoshannah would finish his tunic and give it to her mother-in-law, who had mentioned she was going to visit Mary in two months' time. Mary could pass along her gift to Yeshua, the gift of a grateful bride to the man who had saved her.

- SENECA -

Seneca's helmet was both his bane and his blessing. None of the Jewish dogs who cowered on the pavement in Jerusalem, watching the legions of smart-stepping soldiers march by— legions that inspired terror in small children and women— none of them could know what it was like to wear that helmet. And the men were frightened, too. They were filled with the kind of bowel-emptying horror that clutches your stomach and tears your innards apart. Even though they behaved with a sort of gruff contempt, Jewish men were terrified for themselves. For their families. For their futures.

Seneca bent to tie the top lace of his sandals, then reached for his belt. He had to be honest—the look he saw in the eyes of the Jewish population both invigorated and shamed him. He hadn't shared this feeling with the rest of his battalion— even with the few men he counted as confidantes—though he sensed some of the younger, untried soldiers felt the same way.

It gave him a thrill to walk with power through the streets of Jerusalem as he ran errands for the prelate. He would flick his red cape behind him, watching dark-eyed, veiled women grab their children and shield them from him, as if he were a monster who lived beneath their beds and would come out late at night. Seneca chuckled. He knew he and his compatriots were the stuff of childhood nightmares, used to scare errant children into being good.

But the men were another story. Seneca looked at them with his icy blue eyes and saw revulsion, contempt, and yes—shame. He and his regiment were reviled with the deepest hatred. These Jews were—what did they call themselves?—the "chosen people." Yet these men and their god couldn't protect their women from the random acts of soldiers who, though disciplined, had been away from home too long. These Judeans couldn't stop the crippling taxes that sliced through their meager incomes. They couldn't stop their children from being born into a sort of servitude that sickened them.

Seneca understood their shame and their hate, the kind of visceral, panic-laden hate that led some men to do crazy things that would only lead to their destruction. He shook his head in bewilderment as he continued to dress. What else but insanity would cause a man to rise up against the Romans? The Jewish rabble had always had their share of zealots, but surely they saw it was hopeless? Was it worth it to end up whipped in the streets, or worse yet, nailed to a tree at the crossroads, suffering an unspeakable death?

Would it not be better simply to live out your lot in life and get along as best you could?

Yet Seneca knew, in the deepest reaches of his heart, that he could not live that way either, if he were in their place.

After fastening his cardinal tunic with a gold, knob-like breastpin, Seneca reached for his helmet. A full twelve *mina* it weighed, and wearing it was almost unbearable on days when the Judean temperatures soared. If that weren't bad enough, Seneca carried a history with him that made the helmet even more uncomfortable.

His mother, while pregnant with him in the rolling hills north of Rome, had vowed to the goddess Venus that if her next child was a son—sane and whole—she would place on him the Mark of Venus and dedicate him to the jealous, green-eyed goddess. Her first son, born five years earlier, had come into the world pink and fat and bursting with life. She and her vineyard-owning husband had never dreamed their children would be anything else, in the way of young parents, so self-assured of good health and fortune. But what followed was a succession of stillbirths, children who breathed only a few days before dying, and one child so monstrously deformed he was left for the wolves in the canyons outside the village of Teramo.

In desperation, Seneca's mother sought the help of the goddess of love and marriage to give her another child, promising to devote this child to her. And so when Seneca was born, breathed freely, and thrived for months following his birth—months so fraught with peril, as fevers from the

Vezzola River wafted upward onto the family's land—his parents brought him, in profound relief, to the temple to be anointed.

The Mark of Venus, the sign that would forever bond him to the goddess, was allowing his hair to grow permanently, not letting a razor touch it. As a young boy, this had been a nuisance to Seneca. He'd wanted to play with his friends, but he was forever brushing his burnished umber locks out of his eyes. He remembered the taunts of his playmates: that he looked like a girl, that he needed ribbons, which they would bring to "decorate" his hair. The older, stronger boys in the neighborhood would yank his tresses when he wasn't looking.

It doesn't work, Seneca mused, *to explain to ten-year-olds that your hair is a sign of devotion to a goddess.* Finally, his mother pulled his hair back and held it in place with pins made of bone. It didn't look any less feminine, but at least it was out of the way.

Seneca gazed into the piece of burnished steel that hung in his private cell, a small privilege not afforded to the rank-and-file soldier. Looking at his reflection, he adjusted his cape and helmet so they sat flawlessly on his tall frame. Once his organization and absolute dependability had been discovered, he had risen quickly in the ranks. His position of aide to the prelate required him to be turned out impeccably at all times.

The Roman army had been good for him, he knew. As a second son, there was little else he could do for an occupation. His older brother would inherit what small bit of land and money was left after their parents died. Seneca had the option of becoming a priest or trying his fortune as a soldier. Having been dedicated to Venus, Seneca was already guaranteed a place at the great temple if he wanted it. But while the sly and capricious goddess oversaw love and romance and marriage, she forbade any of those earthly delights for her male priests. Seneca would have been signing away any right to marriage or a relationship or even a sex life. And so he had chosen the path of a soldier.

He smirked at the irony of his life as he strolled out to report to his superior for the morning's briefings. A scroll to be delivered to the high command a mile away. Checking the progress of the water towers being built at the southeastern side of the city, near the Great Gate. A meeting with traders from Samaria, who had complained about the lax behavior of the guards near the marketplace after many of their stalls were vandalized.

If Seneca had known how much of a monk he would be as a soldier, he might have simply stayed closer to home at the temple instead of signing up for Caesar's rolls. At least that way he would have seen his parents occasionally, when they made the trip to the temple to worship. As it was, he hadn't seen them for two years and probably wouldn't for at least seven or eight more. Seneca had imagined women throwing themselves at his feet, awed by his power and good looks. Instead, he was fortunate if he strolled through the streets without instilling terror in the people he passed.

At least, it was that way before Deborah, he thought. *Deborah has saved me in this hellhole of a country.*

He remembered the nightmarish waves of homesickness that had swept over him after he first joined the regiment. After a year's training in Rome, he had been sent to this godforsaken outpost, surely the scourge of the Empire. He recalled his mother's tears and prayers to the gods, asking why her son was being punished. Why could he not simply guard Rome and its glory?

But the gods were silent, and he was off to Judea, a region everyone knew was troubled and accursed. Constant uprisings kept the army commanders alert. A web of spies reported the latest whisperings to Seneca's superiors—who was amassing weapons in the desert, who had met with whom about an insurrection, who was planning a rally in front of the prelate's palace. Most of these uprisings didn't amount to much, though just a year before Seneca arrived in Judea, fourteen Roman soldiers had been killed when a group of Jewish zealots stormed the barracks late one night. Futile, really. Senseless. The perpetrators had been rounded up in full sight of their families and scourged. Those who had survived the brutal flogging were crucified just outside city limits. And so ended that little affair.

Seneca readjusted his helmet and wondered, for the hundredth time, how he could get out of his religious vow, one he had neither asked for nor approved. It had simply been foisted on him by his parents. The Roman army demanded its soldiers be shaven almost bald, which seemed extreme to those entering the service until they had worn the helmets for a few hours. They soon discovered the cumbersome headpieces were easier to wear and marginally cooler when one's head was clean-shaven. Then there was the issue of lice—horrible, filthy little creatures that made a nest of themselves wherever there was hair on the body. Lice couldn't survive if there was no hair.

And so, after enlisting, Seneca had a problem. He could not risk shaving his head and breaking the vow his parents had imposed on him. To do so meant certain calamity, even death from the possessive goddess. But it was also impossible to wear the attire of a Roman soldier with knee-length hair. After many meetings with the temple priests and his commanders, they'd struck a compromise: The priests gave their grudging approval to Seneca cutting his hair once a year. The legion commanders reluctantly agreed to a shaggy-headed soldier. Not even the fierce, battle-hardened soldiers of Rome were willing to anger the goddess. And so most of the year found Seneca with a messy, lion-like mane. Hair that Deborah loved. Hair she often ran her long, tapering fingers through.

He stopped in his tracks on his way to deliver the scroll to Antony, the commander of the Tenth Legion. It still amazed him that the very thought of her could hit him like a pole to the stomach, almost knocking the breath out of him. It was extraordinary he had found a woman to love him so far from home … and that she would be a Jewess—inconceivable!

How could he love a woman like Deborah, a Jew, one of the "chosen people," as she so smirkingly reminded him, yet feel such revulsion for them as a race? See such disgust in the eyes of her countrymen? How was it possible?

Seneca thought wryly of other soldiers in his battalion who commanded women to their beds, took them unwillingly in a back alley, or spent the little money they had on whores. These acts were frowned upon—not because there was any feeling for the women involved, but because they were seen as a breakdown in discipline. Caesar's soldiers must be ready to obey on command, even unto death. Giving in to the urges of the body was counteractive to their mission and discouraged. Even so, Roman commanders turned a blind eye to liaisons of the flesh as long as they didn't become entanglements. The mere physical act of coupling as a means of release was tolerated. Falling in love with a native woman was out of the question.

That's why Seneca knew he was on shaky ground. Not only had he been able to hide his actions—his errands around Jerusalem allowed much free time—he had shielded Deborah from the criticism and charges that would surely be leveled at a Jewish woman who feared her god. At least he hoped he had. He prayed his high position would shelter her from whatever her barbaric people did to fallen women. And as for himself, if he were found out, he would be put under house arrest and probably beaten.

He'd let himself fall in love with her, and so he should stay away. It was the smart thing to do. Yet Seneca could not stop himself from seeking her out on the merest pretense. He would sooner have cut off his right arm than stop loving Deborah.

He hurried off to Antony's offices, rationalizing that if he rushed through his errands, he might be able to squeeze in an extra hour with her. He could not help but laugh when he remembered how they met. It had been a year ago, when he'd delivered a bag of coins to her in payment for a job her husband had been doing on the newly constructed watchtowers. Ever since Antony had caught an underling soldier stealing from the bags he was supposed to be delivering, Seneca had been entrusted to bring payments to their rightful owner.

He'd stood at her door that day, knocking harshly, helmet at his side under his arm. He had seen Deborah's husband several times at the jobsite—a pudgy, somewhat slow, methodical man who nevertheless had a reputation for excellent work. Who would they find to do the work on the ramparts now? A pity, really. As he knocked, he expected to be met by an equally plain mate. As the door swung open and a woman's face appeared, he was stunned, first by her unusual looks and then by the terror and anger in her eyes.

He took a step backward and floundered for the right words in Aramaic, a language he found incomprehensible and illogical—not like Latin, which was based on rules and rationality.

"I come," he began, and stopped as he saw her frozen fright. He cleared his throat and began again. "I come … to give these to you." And he thrust the bag of coins practically in her face, like a little boy offering up a bouquet of wildflowers to his mother.

Although he could still see the numb fear in Deborah's eyes, he could tell curiosity was beginning to take over. Whether it was simply to get him off her doorstep or because she was curious about his errand, she invited him in.

How awkward it had been at first. It was the first time he had ever been inside a Jewish household. He felt too big for his surroundings and lowered himself on a small stool, like an oversized bird on a perch. He tried to talk of his home and family, but the words were hard to find. He could not stop staring at Deborah's face. She was not beautiful, he decided, but her liquid hazel eyes, glossy dark brown hair, and straight, proud stance made her striking. He knew in that moment he desired her and would do whatever it took to make her desire him in return.

As he left that day, he vowed that the delivery of the payment was not the end, but the beginning. And so it had gone, for more than a year. It was difficult—so difficult—after she had been forced to move back to her parents' home. For many months, he caught glimpses of her at the market, found himself shadowing her footsteps as Deborah traveled from one stall to another, catching her furtive glance as she purchased herbs and ribbons and meat, until he was half sick with longing and lust and desperation.

One day on his way back to the barracks, he cut through the market stable, the place vendors housed their animals. She stepped out of one of the stalls, from behind a young horse colt. Seneca was rushing through the long hallway that divided the animals in their separate pens when she reached out and touched his arm. His soldier's instinct was instantly aroused, and he reeled back, reached for his sword, ready to strike.

Deborah cringed and stumbled back into the stall. "Seneca," she breathed, clutching her heart. When he saw who it was, Seneca's head dropped and his breath came fast.

"Oh, Deborah, don't ever do that to me," he said with a nervous laugh. "You could have found yourself minus a hand—or worse!" He pushed her quickly into the stall, away from any prying eyes. "What are you doing here? It will soon be dark, and you have a long way to go."

Deborah leaned on the piece of tunic that protruded from his breastplate, resting her head as she inhaled his scent, the smell of horses and unwashed wool and masculine sweat.

"I simply can't go on like this," she said in a broken voice. "I have tried to forget you. I have reminded myself of all the reasons this is absolutely impossible, and none of them matter." She raised her head and looked him straight in the face. "I have seen you skulking after me in the market, and I can't take it anymore. I must see you, and you must tell me once and for all—is there anything between us, or am I just spinning fantasies? For if you tell me to go, I will put you out of my thoughts and carry on. But I must know."

Her dewy eyes—that strange mixture of green and brown—pierced him to the soul. Eyes that would brook no dissembling, accept no excuses.

"So I was skulking, was I?" he asked, smiling down at her earnest face. "I'm not sure I'd call it that … I'm not sure I was even there for you … "

Deborah grabbed his hand, angry. "Do not play with me. Tell me now. Tell me what I mean to you."

Seneca felt his heart melt, so relieved that this moment had finally arrived. "Oh, my darling, you are everything to me," he murmured as he wrapped her in his arms and peppered her face, neck, and shoulders with kisses. She continued to look straight at him with those clear, calm eyes, as he laid her down and gently began to undress her.

It had been two months since that day, and their meetings were often hasty and contrived, usually in one of the few animal stalls that were vacant while the vendors were busy selling their wares. Sometimes they met in the grove of olive trees near her home. He was ashamed to treat her this way—pledging his love, then bedding her among the detritus of beasts of burden. Whispering his undying devotion, even as he picked leaves and twigs out of her hair. It was unseemly, even for a Roman soldier in love with a forbidden woman. Deborah deserved better, and they both knew it. But neither was strong enough to stop the trysts, and neither could voice the niggling doubt they felt about what would happen. Surely nothing good could come of this. There was no future, and they both knew it. So why did they continue on a doomed course?

Seneca didn't know, and at that moment, he didn't care. As he hurried through the rest of his errands, he only knew that every joint and bone in his body burned for a woman who could not be his—culturally, ethnically, socially, or religiously. A woman he couldn't have at any price. But if he could steal thirty minutes with her this afternoon, it would be enough.

For now.

- Deborah -

In those brief moments at the edge of sleep, Deborah would forget. Before she opened her eyes—before she realized where she was and what her day held, before the past returned to lie on her chest like a heavy piece of lead—she would revel in the coolness of the morning, in the smell of bread baking in her mother's kitchen. She would pretend she was once again a virgin daughter in her parents' home, with no more responsibilities than hauling water from the well and helping her mother prepare the meals.

But those days were over.

Deborah had once watched Aaron and his apprentice, Moishe, struggle with a piece of lead. They settled it carefully—so carefully—onto the wagon that would take it to their worksite, halting each time the donkey moved impatiently, not willing to endanger the precious metal. Every morning, it felt as if that piece of lead crushed Deborah's chest and head, squeezing her lungs and pinning her shoulders to her mat.

Today was the day she must tell her family.

Deborah pulled herself from her bed, the one she shared once again with her younger sister. Of all the hardships being a young widow had brought, the loss of her privacy was the greatest. Never a moment to herself to catch her breath in the coolness of her room. Never a second to stand at the stove and pretend she was preparing meals for her beloved ... for Seneca. For a man she could never have and who could no longer help her.

She would stand strong today. She had made her choices, and now she must bear the consequences. She dressed meticulously, pulling a clean muslin tunic over her head and slipping on her second-best dress, a dull red she loved—a dress Seneca told her reminded him of crushed cherries. She dragged the bone comb through her long brown tresses and checked the pitcher and bowl on the table in the corner of the room. Her sister had brought warm water, and she gratefully splashed it onto her face, drying with a scrap of linen she recognized as a leftover from her mother's last sewing project.

Once Deborah pulled her hair back and tied it with a kerchief, she was ready. She would maintain her dignity, she vowed, even if she were subjected to humiliation.

Deborah remembered the last meeting she'd had with Seneca. As always, it had been in the stables near the market. Their whole affair had been a series of hasty meetings, quick couplings in the hay, murmured endearments—all so *tawdry*. And just as she'd washed the dirt from her face that morning, on that last day in the stable she'd begun to scrape away the fever that had possessed her ever since she'd laid eyes on Seneca. With a clear mind, she could look at their relationship for what it was.

Had she loved him? Oh yes, and she believed he'd loved her as well. But it had been doomed from the beginning, and neither had cared. She had flouted her family, her faith, and her traditions with impunity. The only problem was she had much more to lose than Seneca.

He'd been running one of his numerous errands around the city, and Deborah had waylaid him on the route he usually took across the market square. Immediately, he'd known something was different, something was wrong. He pulled her into the stable, finding an empty stall and clasping her shoulder.

"What is it?" he demanded, his eyes boring into hers. "Something isn't right … ?" He phrased it as a sort of question, taking in Deborah's face, her eyes, her hands, which were clutching the waistline of her dress, dampening it in her sweating fists.

She met his gaze calmly, her red eyes and clumped lashes the only evidence she'd wept all night. She measured her words carefully.

"Seneca, I am fairly sure I am with child," Deborah said quietly. And though she didn't give voice to it, her eyes asked what he intended to do about it.

Seneca's arm fell from her shoulder, and he took a step back. For the rest of her life, she would remember his gaping mouth, the bewilderment in his eyes. In that moment, Deborah's one flicker of hope was snuffed out, for she knew exactly what Seneca would do about it. That step toward the door said more than a thousand words.

He would do nothing.

"And you're sure it's not...? No, it couldn't be your husband's child," he rasped.

"Of *course* not," she snapped. "He died a *year* ago. And anyway, he couldn't—we never could ..." She stopped. She had shamed the memory of Aaron the Mason enough as it was. She would not speak of their dashed marital hopes and dreams to Seneca.

He simply stared at her, his mouth still agape, and Deborah felt the most ridiculous laughter bubble to her lips. The great Roman soldier, aide to the prelate, a man who stood before crowds speaking warnings and supplications and whatever else the Roman government wanted the Jews to know—this great orator could say *nothing*. A *nothing* Jewess had brought him to this state. In that moment, she hated him almost as much as she'd once loved him.

The old story of Amnon and Tamar leapt to mind—how he had loved her with an all-consuming lust until he'd raped her. Then he'd hated her as passionately. It struck her as she stood in the muck of an animal stall—the light streaming through the window, dust motes dancing in the air—how tangled human emotions were. Love and hatred were not far from each other at any time. She couldn't say she truly hated him. She felt ... only ... a sincere disgust.

"I do not expect anything," she continued, not letting him drop his eyes from her face. "I simply came to tell you." She began to push past him, to leave the stall, but he grabbed her elbow.

"But ... but ... what will happen to you?" he stuttered. "Your family ...?"

Deborah stood in stony silence. She would not discuss her family with him.

Then another thought seized Seneca. "I've seen those crowds, those priests of yours stoning people in the streets. It's barbaric, I tell you. Surely—surely that couldn't happen to you?"

Deborah felt a cold shiver go down her spine, but it steeled her confidence. "You dare to speak to me of *barbaric*?" she sneered with a wry laugh. "You impale people on wooden crosses for daring to speak a word against the almighty Romans—a horrible way to die that takes many hours. At least when our people stone someone, it's over quickly and it's because ... because they have *sinned*."

Seneca took in her words with disbelief.

"*Sinned*?" he spat. "For a man and a woman to find some pleasure in each other's arms? Surely you can't believe we have sinned. You can't believe all that nonsense your religion dishes out. You can't be that old-fashioned."

"As a matter of fact, I am," Deborah replied lightly, and just confessing it made her feel better. "I have sinned, and furthermore, I have disgraced my family. And I don't know what will happen to me, but I trust Hashem will provide me answers."

Easy words, glib words, spoken with more bravado than she felt. But in the back of her mind, she thought of those poor wretches cowering on the plain of Ezrishim outside town, waiting for the stone that would knock them senseless ...

Surely not. That would not happen. Her father would not let that happen.

Deborah pushed past Seneca out of the stall, not looking back. She had walked ten paces, willing herself to keep going, to not turn around, when she heard his anguished voice call her name. Stopping, she closed her eyes and let him catch up with her. Seneca had removed his helmet, and the umber hair she so loved was blowing in the breeze. Somewhere, dimly, she thought she should not be seen with him in public, that it would ruin her. Then she realized how ludicrous that was. She was already ruined, and it didn't really matter who saw her anymore. They would know soon enough.

Seneca was fumbling in the pack he carried on his shoulder, pushing a small bag of coins at her, a bag considerably smaller than the one he had proffered the day he came to pay for Aaron's work.

"You must understand I can do nothing," he said, begging her to believe him, grasping her hands in his own. "If I were to own this, I would be severely punished. I might even lose my position and be forced back into the rank-and-file guard!"

Deborah looked at him blankly, and when she didn't seem to comprehend, Seneca's tone turned angry.

"You can't expect me to do anything, Deborah. You knew the risks when we started this."

Deborah shook her head in disbelief. "Oh yes, I knew the risks, and I was a fool," she said softly. She looked at the bag of coins, reached out, took Seneca's hardened hand—double the size of her own—and plopped the bag into it. It looked pitifully small in his palm.

"I don't need this," she said, looking him square in the eye. "I don't need your guilt money." And she strode away, shoulders back, head up, feeling his gaze boring into her back as she went.

Now, as she reached for the sandals beneath her bed, she admitted what an act she had put on that day. She wasn't brave. She was a coward, and only her pride had kept her from groveling at Seneca's feet. Not that it would have done any good, she realized. He was a bigger coward than she. For all his hauteur—his mighty Roman helmet and cape that struck fear into the crowds, his magnificent speaking skills—he was a worm. And the thought made her sick, a wave of nausea sweeping over her and whatever was inside her.

Deborah had never thought of the thing growing in her as a child. That would make it too hard to imagine her future, what it held. Would it be possible to love a child who was part of such a cowardly and despicable man? Would she see those traits in their child? Would the child even be allowed to be born? Seneca's words echoed through her mind.

"I've seen those crowds, those priests of yours stoning people in the streets ... "

She would not think of that. Not right now. One day at a time. Deborah uttered a prayer under her breath as she laced up her sandals.

"Lord of Hosts, Yahweh-Nissi, be my banner. Fight for me, even in my disgrace. Fight for my child."

As she descended the stairs, she took in the scene below. It was so ordinary. Her mother clucked at her younger brother as she stirred the barley porridge, nagging him to bring in water from the large pots outside the door. The family goat, ready to be milked, had once again worked her way out of her pen and was sticking her curious neck inside the door. Yes, a perfectly ordinary day.

Perhaps the last one this family will know, Deborah thought.

"Has Father left for the fields yet?" Deborah asked in a clear voice as her mother threw bowls onto the table. Dear, dear Mother. Short, heavy, slow-moving Mother, whose only thoughts were of food and clothing and keeping her family running. To bring this trouble on them was so wrong, so wicked, and she repented of it in her heart, her mind, her soul ... even before they knew the truth.

Deborah's mother didn't look up. "No, he had to tend to the donkey first, but he'll be leaving soon. Why?" When her daughter didn't respond, the older woman looked up from the table she was setting.

"I need to talk to both of you," Deborah said evenly, and she saw her mother's eyes light up.

Oh no ... she could read her mother like a scroll. She thought Deborah was going to accept the numerous marriage proposals that had come from Nahor's son, Hamamm. *That* would never happen, Deborah vowed, even to hide her disgrace. She would never consent to marry a man with clammy hands and a large pink tongue he constantly ran around his lips. He was revolting. No, no matter what happened in the days to come, she would *not* marry Hamamm.

The memory of the next few minutes would be forever seared on Deborah's heart. When her father returned and finished his breakfast, Deborah sent her younger siblings outdoors and pretended not to see the knowing smirk on her mother's face or the conspiratorial wink she sent her father. As Deborah sat them down, she searched for the right words, then decided simply to say it.

"I am with child."

Her father's stunned face slowly turned into a sort of patronizing, fatherly benevolence.

"Debree, I—I can't say this is good news, but we will handle the wedding preparations quickly and quietly. Hamamm will acknowledge the child. I will meet with Nahor today ... "

"No, Father." Deborah's words were final. "The child is not of Hamamm."

If an itinerant painter had visited their home in that moment, he could not have produced a better still-life tableau. Finally, her mother reached out and took Deborah's hand.

"Then ... who?" she trailed off, faltering. "It couldn't possibly be Aaron ... "

Deborah took a deep breath and sent up a prayer. "His name is Seneca." She looked at their uncomprehending faces, watched them search their memories for a Jewish man with such a strange name, failing to find one. The truth would never occur to them. Ever.

"He is a Roman soldier, Mother."

For a full ten seconds, they stared at her in disbelief. Then her father slumped forward, as if he had been hit in the stomach. Deborah reached out and grabbed him, instinctively massaging her hand over his heart.

"Father, Father, it will be all right," she murmured, taking the role of the parent. "Breathe, just breathe, Father."

Her mother still had not fully comprehended what was happening. She stood frozen, looking as Deborah had always supposed Lot's wife had when she turned to salt—surprised, chagrined, unbelieving. Then suddenly, she grabbed Deborah by the arm, pulled her to her feet, and took her in her arms.

"My poor, poor child," she wailed loudly. "The Romans just take what they want and leave behind the disgrace for us to deal with! And there cannot be any justice for a poor Jewish girl who has been taken by force! May El Shaddai curse him and all of them … "

Deborah pulled away and grabbed her mother's hands, speaking softly and staring into her distraught face. How easy it would be to pretend. To slip into a marriage that would cause some talking and laughing and counting on fingers about the child born too soon. How easy it would be to pretend she had been dishonored by a Roman soldier—a defenseless widow left on her own and taken against her will in a horse stall. But she would not do that to the memory of what she and Seneca had once had. Or to the child she was now carrying.

"Mother, quiet, sssshhh … " Deborah calmed her, speaking softly. "I was not taken against my will. I—I thought I loved him … "

Her mother stood in stunned silence, realization hitting her like a thunderclap. Her mouth hardened into a thin line, her hand snapped up, and she slapped Deborah savagely across her mouth.

"How *dare* you do this?" she hissed. "You have chosen to shame all of us, to bring disgrace on yourself, to carry a bastard child, and to break the laws of God!" She looked at her daughter in disbelief, as if she had grown three eyes or deformed features. "Did we not teach you right from wrong? Were we not there for you when Aaron died? Did we not take you back into our home?"

Deborah could not speak, letting her mother rage. She looked up and saw that her father had been inching himself back toward the door, as if by fleeing he could deny this had ever happened. His mouth was open, and he was breathing heavily. He still had said nothing.

Deborah took a breath and released it, trying to keep her head clear and stem the rising blood that darkened her cheeks and made her feel faint. "I ask for your forgiveness and for the forgiveness of the El Elyon, the God of Hosts," she said quietly, clearly. "More than that, I cannot do."

Her mother was beyond hysteria. "And just what do you think is going to happen when the elders at the gate hear about this?" she screamed. "When the Pharisees get wind of this? Do you think you'll be able to get out of it? With no one stepping forward to claim you as a bride? You are ruined— forever!" Her hand flew to her mouth, as if something had just occurred to her, and she waddled forward and grabbed Deborah by the shoulders, too out of control to speak with any tact or discretion. "Deborah, they could *stone* you! They could *kill* you in the streets!"

Deborah shook off her mothers' red, work-hardened hands, turned, lifted her chin, and ascended the stairs. As she entered the room she shared with her sister, she kicked off her sandals and primly walked over to her mat. She knelt on it as if she were making up the bedclothes for the day, then prostrated herself, her stomach still flat and soft. Raising her arms above her head, she lay utterly still except for the sobs that racked her body. She cried for the death of her love for Seneca. For the death of her relationship with her parents. For the death of her rightness with Yahweh, a Creator she had been taught to love and revere since birth.

And deep in her heart, she cried for what could very well be her own death.

- Maret -

Never had a journey seemed so long. But then, Maret sighed, never *had* a journey been this long—for her, at least. This wasn't a few hours from Cyrene to the village down the road to buy pottery or fine linens. This journey was the culmination of many years' planning, the realization of the hopes and dreams of an entire village.

And it had been a nightmare from the first.

Simon, with his methodical planning, had accounted for several extra days for any sickness or injuries or swollen rivers. If nothing happened, they would be at the outskirts of Jerusalem several days before the start of the Passover—days they could use to wash their travel-worn clothing, eat a meal that wasn't rushed, and yes, even sleep more soundly. Once they reached Jerusalem, they would join the other bands of pilgrims camping outside the city gates and sleep in relative safety.

But the extra time they'd so carefully planned had been quickly swallowed. First, they waited for days by the banks of the overflowing Nile, a river that was always full this time of year but had become unusually swollen by heavy spring rains. After three days of badgering the boatmen for predictions—"When do you think we can go? Is there anyone willing to make the trip across?"—Simon found one willing old man, racked by a muscle disease that twisted his hands into gnarled stumps. He demanded ten *shekels* to take them, their belongings, and their donkey across. A thief. A robber to demand that much, but Simon was desperate to keep going.

Maret prayed without ceasing during the hour-long journey across the Nile. On the rickety boat, she clutched her sons close and expected to be swamped at any moment. The poor, broken-down skiff rode low in the water, and her boys' eyes grew to the size of pot lids when they saw crocodiles in the middle of the river, just a few yards out of reach. The pilot of the boat—not the old man who, despite his ancient appearance, could probably navigate the river better than any other captain—was a boy hardly older than her own Rufus, who struggled with the twelve-foot oar. Maret was sure they would all be plunged to a murky death.

By the time they bumped against the opposite shore and unloaded their possessions, Maret was shaking so hard she could barely lift her parcels. Simon stepped off the skiff with a grim look of determination and quickly moved off into the swampy reeds along the river, where Maret heard him retching.

That evening they had the first of their fights, all the more earth-shaking to Maret because they so seldom quarreled.

And never in the presence of the boys. But that night, with the firelight casting jumping shadows on his face, she berated Simon for planning so poorly, for paying so much for the river fare, for bringing their sons along.

Simon threw up his hands in resignation. "Would you have considered going on this trip without the boys?"

She thought for a moment and replied with honesty.

"No."

"And would you have considered letting me go without you and the boys?"

Maret tossed her gritty, sand-filled wrap around her shoulders and covered her head and the bottom part of her face. She said nothing as she turned away.

That had been the first of several evenings they slept apart—she wrapped up with the boys near the fire, Simon keeping watch some yards away with the donkey.

Two days later, Alexander began complaining of pains in his stomach. Soon his bowels turned to water and they were stopping every half hour for him to find a bush along the roadside. None of the rest of their family was afflicted, but Alexander quickly grew weaker. Soon he was slumped over the donkey, unable to hold up his head. The heat of the desert was droning, unending. They shielded his head with a scarf, they plied him with all the water he could drink, but his eyes were empty and feverish.

"None of the medicines I brought with me are helping," Maret cried in desperation to her husband. "We must stop and let him get better."

That evening, nestled among a rare grove of palm trees and man-sized boulders, Simon and Maret made a small home for their family. They tied blankets between the rocks and laid their mats underneath for the sick boy. Simon waylaid every passenger on the road, asking if they had herbs, medicines, anything that could help a boy who was losing too much water.

Finally, he returned to their grove with a small vial of evil-smelling liquid. "An old Syrian woman said it will help his bowels," he said, handing it to Maret. "But from the way it smells, I'm not sure it will help anything."

Maret didn't want to know what it had cost or consider the possibility they might have been fooled with a potion of river water mixed with herbs. She lifted Alexander's head and realized just how sick he was when he swallowed half the contents of the vial without murmuring. He was the pickiest of her household and refused to eat anything strange or unknown.

Alexander grew stronger, and by the third day they were once again ready to journey onward. Maret stashed the rest of the vial and its precious contents away in the bottom of her medicine bag, praying they wouldn't need it but making sure it was there if they did.

The next few days were blessedly uneventful. For two days they traveled with another young couple and their small girl, but that family turned off in Jordan. *It is amazing,* Maret thought, *how the road provides instant camaraderie.* You didn't ask about a fellow traveler's personal life or religion or political leanings, or if you did, it didn't seem to matter. After a while, everyone became so starved for the sight and sound of other humans they melded into one great traveling mass.

For one night in the desert, they stopped near the campsite of a group of Bedouin traders, rough men with a strange and guttural language. Their women scurried about preparing meals as the men sat around the fire. As Simon and Maret set up camp that evening, she noticed a young girl—heavily pregnant—among the Bedouin group. She couldn't have been more than eleven or twelve. *Too, too young to be carrying a child,* Maret thought, though she knew the desert peoples married their children off even younger than they did in Cyrene.

That night, the girl went into labor and Maret sat at her fire, listening to the poor creature's strangled screams and piteous moans. She hated the men laughing around their campfire and passing a flask of strong drink. She wondered which of these filthy bastards had impregnated that little girl. At one point, she went to Simon and said she couldn't take it anymore—she would go to the girl's tent and see if she could help.

Simon grabbed her by the arm. "Let it be, love," he chided gently. "They have their own women and their own ways."

Seeing the look of horror on Maret's face, he wrapped her in his arms and kissed her gently, placing his hands on each side of her face so her ears could no longer hear the torture in the neighboring tent.

Maret melted into him, the fatigue and worry and grief of the entire trip making her as limp as the old rag toy Rufus had carried around as a baby.

"Just leave it to Yahweh," Simon crooned over and over, soothing her into a kind of trance. Finally, he led her to her mat, where she tossed fitfully for the next several hours, drowsing in a kind of netherworld nightmare. A land between worlds—between her good, solid home in Cyrene and this desert of grief.

When dawn broke, she startled upright and realized she heard nothing. Silence ruled the camp. Maret fell back onto her mat, thanking Yahweh the girl's ordeal was over. But when she did not hear the lusty cries of a healthy newborn, or even the mewling gurgles of a sickly one, she knew that not only was the girl's trial over, but the baby's was too. It had not seen the light of day. And of the girl?

If Elohim is merciful, He will take her, too, she thought bitterly. *Otherwise, she'll be in the same condition a year from now.*

Oh, she hadn't always been so cynical, so bitter. This trip had hardened her, pulled her from the safety and security of her home, from her position as a mother of two strong, healthy boys and wife of a well-respected citizen of Cyrene. It had thrust her into a reality of pain and suffering and heartbreak. And she didn't want it! Even though it was the trip of a lifetime, she didn't want to see this side of the world. She wanted to be sheltered like a child.

Maret prayed things would change once they reached Jerusalem. Oh, surely they would! The City of David, the home of God's elect, the city of Zion!

The words of the well-known Psalm filled her mind: "*I rejoiced with those who said to me, 'Let us go to the house of the Lord.' Our feet are standing in your gates, Jerusalem.*"

Yes, once they got to Jerusalem, everything would be better. Surely their luck would change.

- Seneca -

For at least the tenth time that night, Seneca thought through his options again. *Options*. That word was laughable when he felt like a rat in a trap. Did he have options? Truly? Or was this fruitless list-making just a waste of time?

He could go to his commander and ask to be released from the army so he could marry a Jewish woman. Even as he finished that thought, he knew how ridiculous it was. *Ask to be released*. Ludicrous. Only once in all his years with the Roman army had a soldier been released, and the man had obviously been insane. Shipped back home and kept in an asylum the rest of his life. Soldiers weren't "released." If their conduct was so bad it was detrimental to the rest of the platoon, they were executed. Quickly. Quietly.

To marry a Jewish woman. Seneca snorted, his chest filled with pain and wonder at his own stupidity. That would never happen, *could* never happen, in a million years. Even if he did marry Deborah, how would a former soldier find acceptance in a backwater village where the crowds were frightened silly at the sight of him? He knew a few Romans in higher authority kept Jewish wives—quietly, on the side—and it was overlooked. The woman had to be willing to give up her life and family and eventually move with her husband to Rome. But he was nowhere near the echelon that would allow him such freedom.

One other thought flitted about the edges of Seneca's awareness, digging into his psyche even as he kept pushing away: *Confess to his superiors and take the punishment.* He would openly admit his affair with Deborah and take responsibility for the child. There would be no possibility of marriage, though he could pay for the child's support aboveboard—no slipping a few coins into Deborah's hand when he happened to see her.

But what exactly would his punishment be? That was the crux the whole matter hinged on. At the very least, he would be beaten—not savagely flogged like those poor animals in the streets who tried to thwart the Roman government—but beaten with wooden canes until he was black and blue. As miserable and humiliating as that prospect was, he could live with it. But what would become of his position with the prelate? He would not, *could* not, debase himself by entering a platoon again as a foot soldier. He had worked too hard, clawing his way up the ladder of responsibility. A fall from grace would mean starting over.

Seneca pushed away the scrap of paper he had been writing on, jotting down phrases or words, adding and subtracting what his salary would allow. As he glanced down, he saw the most prevalent thing on the page was the word "Deborah," scribbled over and over. He crumpled the sheet up and flung it across his cell, where it landed on his bed.

Pacing back and forth, he forced himself to think about this last possibility. His relationship with Deborah would be recognized and the child ascribed to him. He would be able to support it, maybe even see it occasionally. He stopped abruptly. For the first time, it occurred to him that Deborah might not want that. What if she rushed into another marriage to cover up their affair? Surely she wouldn't face the wrath of her people and her god alone? How could she accept the shame of everyone knowing she had fallen in love with a hated enemy of the Jews?

If Seneca were demoted, would he even have enough salary to help her and the child? Would she accept the money, even if he did? What, what, *what* was happening with her and her family? Would they keep a fallen woman in their midst? Or would she be turned over to the religious authorities who walked the streets of Jerusalem with their noses in the air, as if they always smelled something bad? Surely Deborah's fate wouldn't rest with them?

It had been a week since Deborah waylaid him in the stables, a week of his mind churning like the rapids of the Lower Jordan River. He remembered marching along its banks when his company first arrived in Palestine. A deceptive river, the Jordan. Wide and placid in places, wild and buckling in others. Once, they'd taken a rest in a place where the water was smooth but swift, lapping like dogs and heaving handfuls of water over their sweating heads and faces. Farther down, the surging stream hit a large rock in the middle of the water. The current became divided, cutting the expanse into two smaller rivers that sprayed foam on the boulder, then merged again five paces later.

Seneca felt his life was like that stream, headed toward the rock he'd known all along was there but hadn't heeded. Now that he'd hit it, circumstances divided him from Deborah, and he couldn't see them coming together again. It was through. He'd been thrown against the rock and stranded.

Seeing no answers, Seneca finally gave up and fell into a fitful sleep. In the morning, he pulled on his cape and stood up straight. He had work to do for Tyrus, his prelate—a report to deliver across the city and a meeting with several other centurions who were bringing forth complaints from their troops about vendors in the marketplace overcharging the men.

Wily bunch, the Judeans, Seneca thought with a wry smile. *We rule them, but they'll make us pay for it,* denarius *by* denarius.

As he strode into his superior's office across the compound, a thought struck him for the first time. His child wouldn't just be Judean. It would be half of him, half his blood. He envisioned his mother—how she would love cradling a baby in her arms! If only he could take Deborah to his family, they would love and accept her; he knew they would. The thought of a child with his eyes and mane of hair made Seneca grow dizzy.

Boulder or not, how could he let himself be cut from his child's life?

The meeting wore on with the usual litany of complaints—the soldiers were being taken advantage of in the market, though they couldn't prove it. The vendors were rude and unhelpful. A few small boys had thrown rotten pieces of fruit at two soldiers.

"It's not worth stirring everyone up to make a show of things," Seneca's superior wisely advised. "Ignore it. Let them alone. The might of Rome isn't going to be turned against some disgruntled vendors. We have bigger matters to attend to."

The centurions left in disgust, hoping to be given authority to make examples of the troublemakers. But those higher up in the Roman army had long ago learned to choose their battles. Though they technically ruled, an entire hierarchy had been put into place, which included the religious leaders, the Pharisees and Sadducees, whose arguments turned in circles and made Seneca's head ache. You never could get a straight answer out of any of them. And then there was Herod, slimy little worm that he was, placed by Caesar as a puppet ruler. Everyone knew he didn't have much real power—at least nothing Rome hadn't given him—but he had to be consulted when decisions were made, to save face. The less Herod was brought into the mundane troubles of the troops, the better off everyone—both Jews and Romans—would be.

Seneca picked up the report he was to deliver to the Roman across the city. It dealt with an aqueduct that was supposed to be built to bring water in through the Sheep's Gate, something the Jews had been demanding for years. It was a poor side of Jerusalem, and the people there had to travel almost half a mile to get water. The aqueduct would save them many trips and hours during the heat of the day. A show of goodwill, a bone thrown to the conquered to keep them contented—for a little while, at least.

Placing his helmet firmly on his head and tying shut the clasp that held his cape together, Seneca left the military post on the northeast side of the city and headed west. For several blocks, the sights and sounds of a miniature Rome enveloped him. He was passing through the quarters where the highest of the Roman officers lived, raised their families, and ruled over households of servants, some of them brought from home. He smelled fresh oregano being ground for the spicy flatbreads the Romans loved so much—an herb transported at great cost from Tuscany. Seneca remembered Tyrus talking about his wife trying to grow the herb here in Judea.

"But the soil here doesn't amount to anything," Tyrus had said. "It'll only support some goats and sheep … a few olives … and rebels." He'd laughed with his mouth open, head back, straight white teeth flashing. If the Romans wanted the comforts of home, they had to pay dearly for them.

Seneca was traveling light today. Sometimes, when he was laden with documents and bags that had to be delivered across the city, he pressed a local boy into service to carry for him. He had that right, though the Jews hated them for it. Some of the soldiers took advantage of the locals, making them haul bundles of firewood or hay for their steeds. After a mass of Temple officials had complained to Tyrus, a guideline was put into place: A conquered person could be required to carry a load for a Roman soldier up to a mile and no more. And occasionally Seneca invoked the rule, hauling in a teenage boy to carry bundles or a younger boy to tote scrolls that weren't overly important. It was good for them to remember who they were … and who the Romans were.

After a mile, he came into the precincts of the Temple. Huge and whitewashed, this imposing building rivaled any of the temples of Seneca's homeland. He remembered the temple of Poseidon so close to his home, with its marble pillars and sea-blue draperies. Seneca had never been stationed near the Temple courtyards in Jerusalem, though some soldiers were routinely on duty to make sure the masses stayed under control.

The sight of the noonday sun blazing on the Temple's snow-white walls gave Seneca a sick feeling in the pit of his stomach. Everything that had to do with the Jews reminded him of her. Of them. Of the woman he'd thought he loved and the child she now carried. He would have to decide soon what he was going to do … before Deborah did something that made the decision for him.

Or maybe that's what he was waiting for? If he were very honest with himself, maybe he knew that by doing nothing, the decision would be made. Nothing would happen to him, and Deborah would either marry someone else or bear the consequences of her god and her people.

Maybe I am a coward, he thought angrily, kicking a bundle of rags some woman had evidently dropped on her way back from the laundry tubs. It would be better for her to marry again. She wouldn't want to live off the charity of her family forever. No matter the culture, no one wanted to keep an unattached woman in their home, supporting her when she could be foisted off in marriage to someone who would take her while she was still young.

The low bellowing of animals was barely discernible above the noise of the streets. Seneca hoped to avoid the up-close doings of the Temple, so he took an alternate route below the imposing structure. One time he had been compelled to cut across the Court of the Gentiles—a shortcut from the Mount of Olives to the middle of town—and had been appalled by what he'd seen and smelled. Vendors hawking their wares, yelling loudly to catch the attention of passersby, even as those who wanted to pray stood just feet away. Money changers transferring *denarii* into the Temple *shekel*, gouging you for your efforts. Animals milling about uneasily, lowing in fear and anxiety; small boys herding them across the floor of the Temple courts to the slaughtering pens.

Seneca could not understand a religion like this. Yes, animal sacrifice was part of his culture as well, but the animals were purchased miles away and brought to the temple in a civilized manner. No one was expected to pray while dodging piles of dung underfoot. It never ceased to amaze him that the Pharisees—that religious class of men who were monumental pains in the neck—condoned this circus.

Deftly avoiding the Temple by maneuvering through the squalid Lower City, Seneca wondered why the lanes and alleys were so empty. Usually at this time of day, children were kicking balls against the houses or hurrying to late-morning schooling, books tucked under their arms. Women were usually returning from the well with jars of water balanced precariously on their heads. Yet other than an old, sightless beggar who moaned and crouched along the side of the street, hand outstretched, no one was going about their business.

Odd . . .

A man's raised voice caught his attention, coming from a street over. When Seneca stopped to listen, cape swirling about him, he realized there was more than one voice—all of them the baritone and bass rumblings of men. One, shriller than the others, was clearly upset and trying to make a point. *Not a good sign*, he thought. He wondered for a moment if he should go and find help, but there were no Roman outposts in this part of the city. He would see what was happening first—perhaps it was only an escaped animal that the men were trying to corral. No sense in raising the alarm if that were the case.

Seneca continued on his way, pulling himself upright and placing a protective hand on the sword at his side. Usually just the sight of a Roman soldier stopped these riffraff in their tracks. They would disperse voluntarily, even if they still mumbled curses under their breath.

As he came around the corner, Seneca wasn't prepared for the scene that met his eyes at the end of the thoroughfare. Angry men, eyes tightened in fury, gesticulating, mouths wide open, hissing and shouting—all of them facing what looked like a pile of cloth on the edge of the street ... if it could properly be called a street. Truly it was more like an alley, an unpaved byway with a dusty dead-end wall. The only way out of its narrow straits was to go back the way he had come. Seneca knew it was dangerous to be trapped this way, but he wanted to get a handle on the situation before raising an alarm.

To his dismay, four Pharisees stood in a group in the middle of the lane, their rich clothing contrasting sharply with the plain, homespun fabrics of the rest of the men. Their presence alone spelled trouble. As he stood and watched, Seneca was struck by how calm the Pharisees were compared to the rest of the men—and it was, he observed, all men. The women and children must have been cowering in their houses until this spectacle—whatever it was—had passed. Once again, it seemed the Pharisees had stirred up the people while remaining aloof and smirking themselves.

Masters of troublemaking, he thought.

The bundle of cloth in the street shifted a little. Was it the wind? Or was there something inside? Surely it wasn't ... a person? Seneca edged forward, still unnoticed by the rabid crowd. Then he saw another man step forward out of the throng and make his way into the street. He was dressed simply in the plain, rough-hewn tunic of a laborer. He was taller than most of the men and striking in the ruddiness of his cinnamon-colored skin. Obviously, he spent a great deal of time out of doors. Suddenly, the Pharisees noticed the man and fastened their attention on him.

"Why did you call me here?" the man asked, stretching out his hands as if to prove he had nothing to offer them. The situation began to make more sense to Seneca. Whatever was in that bundle must belong to the man in the street, though why that should provoke such anger from the crowd—or the necessity of any crowd at all—perplexed him.

One of the Pharisees—whose purple tunic marked him as a leader in the Temple—stepped forward, looking pointedly at his feet to make certain he did not step in a pile of animal dung. He lifted his hem to hold it above the filth of the street and made his way over to the newcomer.

"We have asked you to come because we have a point of Law we care to discuss with you," pronounced the Pharisee, as if he were conferring a great honor on the lowly man. Seneca couldn't understand what was happening—the man was obviously a laborer, not a learned rabbi. Why would a bunch of religious men who thought they were too good for everyone want the opinion of a commoner—unless they were being sarcastic? Perhaps the point was to humiliate him.

The man said nothing as he waited for the Pharisee to continue. He had a sort of dignity, Seneca thought, that was not diminished by the crowd's screaming or the priest's questioning. This was going to be an interesting conversation.

Seeing that the man would say nothing more, the Pharisee dropped his lofty tones and expressed himself with some urgency. He gestured at the pile in the street, almost ten feet away from them.

"This woman has been caught red-handed in the act of adultery," he announced to the crowd, whose frenzied booing and hissing became louder. "She has been the widow of Aaron the Mason for many months, his memory be preserved." In an act of pious devotion, the Pharisee reverently dropped his eyes.

As if he cares one whit about the memory of Aaron the Mason, Seneca thought bitterly. *Some poor man who was probably so far beneath these hypocrites ...*

And then Seneca's head snapped up. *Aaron the Mason? How many could there be? And even if there was more than one, could they both be dead? Surely that pile on the street, that lump of clothing wasn't ... Deborah?* He gasped even as his feet were frozen to the stones where he stood.

The Pharisee went on. "Even though her husband of blessed memory has been dead for many months, she is newly expecting a child. And even though her family has tried to preserve their good name, not to mention"—here the man raised a finger—"the good name of this woman, by marrying her to a willing and stable man, she has refused."

The gasps of the crowd grew louder, the voices more accusatory.

He's enjoying this, Seneca thought. That little son of a jackass was enjoying this whole demonstration, whipping up the crowds and humiliating this woman who, though he refused to acknowledge it, could be Deborah. Seneca's stomach moved into his throat at the very thought.

The Pharisee raised his voice and went on. "The Law of Moses is very clear: This woman should be stoned. But you, Teacher, seem to have a solution for everything … so what do *you* say?"

The man in the street had been standing quietly, observing the crowd, listening to the Pharisee. When the Pharisee finished his speech, everyone turned to watch what this man, this teacher, would say. He let them stand in total silence for a moment, then walked over to the pile of cloth in the street and reached his hand down, touching it. The thing—the woman—flinched, but the man pressed his hand down harder, motioning her to stand, pulling her up.

Suddenly, the woman's face and shoulders rose. She had been on her knees, bent forward, completely covered from head to toe by the robe and headpiece she wore. And in that moment—in that *awful* moment—Seneca saw her.

It was Deborah.

In the name of all the gods, she was dirty and her face was tear-streaked—he could see that even from a distance. As she rose, he saw her headpiece was askew and her hair—that beautiful, glossy, brown hair—was slipping out from beneath it. He wanted to lunge forward, draw his sword, and rip open the smug, religious men standing there. He wanted to chop the accusing crowd to pieces, their stench of anger and hate so strong he could smell it even from where he stood. But for the life of him, Seneca could do nothing. He stood immobile.

Deborah leaned onto the plain man, too weak to stand straight. Releasing her waist, the man bent down and wrote something in the dirt with his finger. No one except Deborah was close enough to read it—what was he doing? Trying to buy some time with the Pharisees? After a few seconds he straightened, again holding Deborah around the waist. She was pale, and her head drooped.

The man's voice was clear and unexpectedly loud. "Tell you what," he said, as if he had just come upon a solution. "There's a pile of building stones down the street. The person who is sinless here—go grab a rock, and you can be the first to throw it."

A look of horror crossed the Pharisee's face. *Whatever he was expecting this teacher to say, that evidently wasn't it,* Seneca thought. His heart ached for Deborah, for her disgrace, for her need to be rescued by someone she didn't even know. He should be the one charging in to take her away. But did he have that right? Romans couldn't interfere in religious doings, even if they seemed barbaric or strange. But he knew, in his heart of hearts, that Deborah was standing there because of him. He was just as much the adulterer as she.

The crowd seemed frozen, as if they all waited for someone else to tell them what to do. He saw several men murmur to each other. A ripple ran through them—one that seemed abashed, almost ashamed to Seneca's ears.

Suddenly, the lead Pharisee, the one in purple, hiked his shoulders back and without another glance at the teacher or the woman in the street, headed Seneca's way. The other three in his group followed uneasily, looking for all the world like a flock of ducklings plodding after their mother. Seneca backed up, searching for a way to retreat without having to run. Several feet away was the tunneled entrance to a small courtyard. He ducked into it, melting far enough into its shadows that they could not see him in the gloom, but he could still watch the procession.

After the religious leader, the men filed past in groups of two and three … quietly, sheepishly. Seneca stayed frozen, waiting for Deborah and this strange man to pass his hiding place, but they did not appear. After several minutes, he emerged from the tunnel and crept back to the corner. Deborah stood facing the man, head almost fallen to her waist as he grasped her shoulders. Suddenly, she fell at his feet, grabbing them with both her hands, kissing and rubbing them gently.

The teacher reached down to stroke her head with a large hand. "Daughter, I do not condemn you. Go on your way. From now on, don't sin."

Even from twenty paces, Seneca could see the incredulity on Deborah's face. Then she was beaming, crying, and trying to talk all at once. She bent down again and kissed the man's feet before he took her by the hand and lifted her up. As they headed Seneca's way, the teacher murmured something to her that Seneca couldn't catch. Once again, he wheeled around and took refuge in the dark passageway until they passed, walking slowly and talking together. Then curiosity took hold of Seneca.

Peeking cautiously both left and right and seeing no one, he strode out of the dark place to the site of Deborah's rescue. It was deserted. The dead-end alley had returned to being a quiet, out-of-the-way place used by builders to store supplies.

Seneca strode the twenty paces to the middle of the dusty street, where he could see the flat outline left by Deborah's body in the dirt. And next to it, he could see the writing the teacher had done with his finger. It was in Aramaic, and as much as that language boggled Seneca for its irregularities and odd constructions, he could read it:

"The Psalmist says, 'The Lord is close to the brokenhearted and saves those who are crushed in spirit.'"

Seneca's eyes filled with tears, and he watched as they fell onto the words in the street, words that were already disintegrating in the gentle breeze. He stood as the sounds of the city resumed—a goat *baaing;* a child's high, excited voice; the staccato cadence of builders hammering nails out of rhythm with each other.

Seneca stood and knew the truth: Deborah had made a decision without him, because he would not make one. He was a coward. He had let her suffer the consequences alone because she was too true to herself to rush into a sham marriage. He had let his pride and his ego and his fear come between him and the woman he loved.

In that moment, Seneca knew who was the conquered and who was the conqueror.

- ELKANAH -

The stench was overwhelming. It permeated the barn and the hay, and it clung to Elkanah's clothing long after he returned home. On days when temperatures reached their peak by noon, the sulfuric fumes threatened to take one's breath away. And the flies were almost worse—the way they landed on the wetness of his arms and face and neck, sucking in the moisture of his sweat.

Unclean. Filthy. Unbearable.

Even after three years of working with donkeys and learning every one of their intimate secrets—the way they lifted their tails and plopped their dung all over the stall but pulled their legs apart and urinated daintily, like little girls—Elkanah never ceased to be disgusted by them. Their breeding habits, their noisy, loud chomping, their incessant and shrill braying—he often wondered how he had found himself in this life.

But it wasn't really a mystery. After all, as his father proclaimed proudly to one and all, the house of Joachim had sold donkeys in Bethphage for years. The family was proud of their stock and had built up quite a business over the past two decades. Not that they were wealthy—no, no—but much better off than the average tradesman. Even so, the stench of shiftiness, the aroma of a shady deal, hung on the family much as flakes of dried dung clung to the bottom of their sandals every time they crossed the courtyard.

The business was a necessary evil in the village. Every family with any means at all occasionally trudged up the slight rise to the home of Joachim ben Rahan to choose a spirited colt as a wedding gift for a favored daughter or an older, better-tempered mare for hauling produce to the market. Though the family's business was needed in Bethphage, Elkanah knew the reputation that surrounded their trade—they were painted as swindlers and crooks, willing to sell a donkey born with a limp as if it simply had a pebble in its hoof and would soon recover.

And in his heart, Elkanah knew the reputation was not unmerited. Though his father brayed almost as loudly as the donkeys he sold about the family's "untarnished" reputation, Elkanah heard the whispers that circulated in the market and the synagogue about his father and his deals.

Yes, the family of ben Rahan was a fixture in the neighborhood, though not necessarily a welcome one.

Elkanah laughed bitterly to himself. The most ironic thing was that he'd despised donkeys since he'd been assigned to haul water and feed to the stables as a little boy. The blasted creatures had sensed his fear. One large, coal-black jack had terrified Elkanah, taking bites out of his wrist with his massive, yellow teeth as the small boy lifted the bucket over the gate. When Elkanah whimpered to his father later, showing the bloody piece of flesh the donkey had torn, Joachim didn't know with whom he was angrier—a dumb beast in his stable, or his own pathetic, sniveling son. He marched Elkanah out to the adjoining stalls and soundly slapped the jack across the nose.

"You need to show him who's the master!" he yelled at his son. "You can't be afraid of him!"

Fear, however, was Elkanah's constant companion. He had never known what it was like not to be afraid—of the bullies at synagogue school who teased him for smelling like an ass; of the donkeys in the stable; of his father, who berated him for his timid ways; of girls in general, and Ruchel, his cousin, most specifically. He knew his parents had their eye on Ruchel as his wife, but Elkanah blanched at the thought. Ruchel—with the lovely, honey-brown hair and voice that set off a humiliating flutter in his stomach every time he heard her speak. Even though Ruchel was kind when they met at family gatherings, he knew what she was thinking: *He's beneath me. I can do better.* And Elkanah could do little but agree.

Elkanah knew he wasn't clever. After all, the smart boys had been snatched by the local rabbis to continue their schooling at age twelve, when synagogue school finished. Even Uncle Isaac hadn't chosen him, much to the chagrin of Elkanah's parents, who wanted at least one learned member of the family. For all the boasting by Elkanah's father about their money and their status and their business, it stung that they were seen as crude and unlearned by the synagogue community. To have a child who was attached to a rabbi—well, that would have been proof enough of their position in society! But after Elkanah's turn came and then went, his parents set their sights on their younger son, Bashel.

And so it was the world of the donkeys for Elkanah, days that seemed to drag on endlessly. Feeding them, cleaning out their pens, selling them to merchants and well-heeled members of the community, sending out the mares to be bred, and always, *always* watching for signs of disease or injury, like punctured hoofs or gut worms.

Even at home he couldn't escape it. Donkeys were all his father could talk about, even when shoveling food into his mouth at the evening meal, spraying his tablemates with saliva—and looking, Elkanah thought, for all the world as if he belonged in the stable, too. Just last night he had lifted his hand, holding a slice of the flat brown bread his mother had baked and pointing it at Elkanah.

"Are you keeping up on that cracked hoof on the little black colt?" he sputtered at the boy. "Keep the ointment on, and if there's pus oozing out, you've got to double the treatment."

"Really, Joachim," his wife scolded. "Must we talk about such things at the table? You'll make everyone ill."

"Nonsense," her husband retorted, turning to her. "I'll never get that colt sold if that hoof doesn't heal. Old Benjamin in the market says the quickest way to cure hoof rot is to get him out of the stall and into the sunshine. Says if he stands in his own shit all day long, it'll never get better."

Elkanah's mother had long since learned to tune out her husband's coarse talk and behavior. She lived a life centered on her home, her children, preparing meals, keeping the freshest herbs and spices in her pantry, and overseeing the servant girls who came in to tend to the laundry. Her husband's manners—or lack of them—no longer concerned her. If donkeys—those filthy, ill-bred beasts—were the means to making her family's life more comfortable, then so be it. She could live with that. Ignoring her husband's outburst, she turned away in silence. Elkanah winced at her submission.

This morning found a sulky Elkanah tending to the black colt's wounded hoof, gently massaging the vile-smelling ointment into the crack. In spite of himself and his disgust of the whole breed, he had learned to love this foal, who seemed to understand he was somehow damaged and would never trot saucily with the others, throwing his head back at a sassy angle. Elkanah knew it sounded ridiculous, and he would never tell anyone, but he sensed a kindred soul in the little animal, whom he had tacitly dubbed Sha-Khohr—Blackie.

The small colt stood patiently, allowing Elkanah's ministrations as if he sensed the boy's camaraderie. After rubbing the thick, yellow, viscous mass into the crack in his hoof and carefully cleaning out the crusty seepage that had accumulated, Elkanah led the docile creature to the wall outside the stable, which backed onto a secondary road leading from Bethphage to Jerusalem. It was a quiet spot, away from the traffic that flowed to the market on the street in front of the house. Elkanah knew too many passing animals, caravans, legions of soldiers, and merchants would scare the little colt, especially when the market road was used by the children heading to synagogue school, who had a penchant for throwing rocks or pulling the tails of donkeys tied up for sale. Keeping Sha-Khohr behind the house, on this quieter road, would protect him. Elkanah tied the colt to the hitch pin sticking out of the wall, planning to leave him out for an hour or so.

Elkanah was in the back of the stable, trying to find an extra bucket to bring the little colt some water, when he heard voices coming from the courtyard. *Probably the traders from Shechem*, he thought, remembering his father mentioning the deal he was trying to strike. Elkanah chuckled as he exited the stable, carefully shutting the wooden door behind him. His father would have his work cut out for him. Merchants from Shechem were known for their shrewd and canny ways, and they would spot one of Joachim's shady offerings from a furlong away. It would be an interesting exchange.

But now Elkanah could see these men in the courtyard, and they were clearly *not* from Shechem. There were two of them, and they wore the coarse, unbleached muslin of those who lived near the Sea of Galilee. Elkanah had seen Galileans only occasionally at the market, when they'd hauled a large catch and sold the excess fish in Bethphage. Everything about them was different—the way they pronounced certain words, their closely trimmed beards, the rope on their sandals.

Elkanah's old fear returned. Living in a world of beasts, he did not do well conversing with strangers. He became tongue-tied, always shuffling his feet and looking at the ground. But these men appeared ill at ease, too. One of them stepped forward, wiped the sweat from his forehead, and took a big breath.

"I know this is going to sound strange ... "

Elkanah stepped back and looked behind him. "I can get my father for you," he blurted out. "He does all the trading on the donkeys."

The man in front took another step forward, reaching out his hand and speaking gently in the soft accent of his region. "No, son, you do not need to bother your father. I'm sure he's very busy. I know this is a strange request, but we need to borrow your little colt here."

He pointed at Sha-Khohr.

"*Borrow* him?" Elkanah's brow furrowed in puzzlement. Occasionally a merchant would rent a donkey for a few days to travel to another village, but Elkanah had never heard of lending one out. "He has a cracked hoof ... he's out here in the sun to help it heal ... if you'll just let me get my father ... "

The second man, who had been silent thus far, stepped forward.

"Our master ... " he stopped, hesitating, then swallowed as if forcing courage into himself. "Our master has need of him," he said, shrugging as he made a motion to untie the black colt.

Elkanah panicked. Sha-Khohr was *his* responsibility, and now it became clear these men were common thieves! And in broad daylight! The fear that lodged like a pit in his stomach turned to anger, and he jumped forward and wrestled the rope out of the second man's hands. The startled colt began to kick and toss his head, sensing something was wrong.

The first man, coming up behind the boy, grabbed Elkanah by his thin shoulders and pulled him away. For a moment, Elkanah fully expected to be stabbed or bludgeoned across the head. He cringed, waiting for the blow to come, but the man gently disengaged him from the small donkey's halter and looked him straight in the face. His hazel-brown eyes were gentle but desperate.

"Listen, son, I don't understand this myself, but my master has need of him," he said in a low, urgent tone. "My—master—has need—of him."

The second man, bigger and burlier than the first, laid his hand on Elkanah's head. "We'll make sure he gets back to you—I promise," he said. "After we're through with him, we'll get someone to take him back. We won't hurt him."

Elkanah stood paralyzed with confusion, fear, and inde-cision as he watched the larger man gently untie Sha-Khohr and rub him behind the ears, one of the colt's favorite spots. He stood there, watching the men walk purposefully down the secondary road, leading the gentle, unbroken colt away. He stood there, watching, his heart pounding, his breath coming fast.

He thought of only one thing. And it wasn't his father's wrath or the probable beating that would follow; it wasn't that he had escaped what he'd thought was an attempted robbery, though he still wasn't so sure he *hadn't* been robbed.

Elkanah's only thought was this: *The only living thing in this world that understands me is being taken away.*

- Isaac -

Isaac arrived at the Temple a little breathlessly, late as usual. His reminiscing about meeting Yeshua had once again gotten the best of him. A long day of work lay ahead, including rewriting the haphazardly scrawled Council notes. A usual morning task the day after the drawn-out, tedious meeting, and one Isaac detested. Because of his low position, he was not allowed to sit in on Council meetings and take the notes himself. Instead, old Malachi handed him sheets of papyrus each week that were covered with ink blots, words scratched through, and a crust of sand where the old priest had hastily tried to dry the writings. Isaac would spend most of the morning deciphering the cryptic scribblings.

There was also the urgent matter of spreading the word through the Temple ranks of his availability as a tutor. He would take more boys into his afternoon session, or if he found favor in the sight of Yahweh, a wealthy family would hire him to teach their son privately.

From the back alley, Isaac he entered the section of the Temple where he ordinarily worked. He immediately noticed an eerie quiet.

Odd, he thought. Usually at least a dozen priests were meeting, sharing family news, assigning tasks, and gathering supplies for their work. But the room was still ... at least within. From outside, Isaac could hear the bleating of animals and cries of peddlers selling everything from sacrifices to food for hungry travelers. Mixed in were the insistent calls of the money changers, each trying to persuade travelers they had the best exchange rate.

Thieves, all of them, Isaac thought. For many years, he had disdained their presence in the Temple, and more than once he'd pondered whether the Jewish faith had become too weighty with rules and regulations—many of which had, after all, not been set down by Moses but evolved from tradition. And tradition, Isaac had long since learned, could be a heavy taskmaster. But a smart man—a man looking for additional tutoring work—kept his thoughts about such matters to himself.

However, today Isaac couldn't seem to let the matter go. Take the Temple *shekel,* for instance. To pay the yearly Temple tax, faithful Jews had to change their money to the *shekel,* a currency only in circulation at the Temple in Jerusalem. It was a sign of faithfulness and purity before God—money from the Roman government would not be accepted. And so, people who had traveled long distances—people who were tired and dusty and hungry—had to find someone to exchange their money. Hence the bellowing sideshow that had erupted in the Court of the Gentiles.

Isaac knew without a doubt those money changers gave terrible exchange rates. They had a monopoly on the business after all—where else could the people go? Even though Isaac had timidly protested their presence to the elder priests, he had finally come to see them as a necessary evil.

And then there was the Court of the Gentiles itself. It was a disgrace. King Solomon had long ago commanded that the Temple have a quiet place of prayer for those who were not ethnically Jewish, but had found Yahweh and worshipped him. They could not, of course, enter the court of Jewish men or women, but this place was supposedly theirs. Nevertheless, the money changers had slowly moved their stalls from the streets outside the Temple into the Court of the Gentiles, and now they refused to leave—just as a dog who is allowed to warm up at a fireplace once will never give up its spot. Isaac shook his head impatiently as he remembered the arguments of the priests: "It's more convenient for the people to have the money changers right there—there aren't that many Gentiles using the court anyhow."

Once the money changers were let in, it was as if a mighty river had diverted course. Soon the food vendors were lighting fires and peddling bread and lamb and rice; the animal sellers were marking out corners of the court for their wares—bringing with them the sounds of frightened creatures and the stench of feces. It was impossible to walk through the court without soiling your sandals, and Isaac avoided it as much as he could.

To make matters worse, the Court of the Gentiles was a perfect shortcut for those hauling items from the city to the Mount of Olives or vice versa. At any time of day, you could be bumped by a man hauling a load of figs, or a pair of children entrusted by their parents to deliver goats' milk to the other side of the city. *Just where exactly is a Gentile supposed to pray?* Isaac often wondered.

It all reminded him of the traveling troupe of Greek actors from Sepharim he had once seen performing a play in the fields outside the city. So many merchants and thieves hanging on the fringes, trying to make a living. He remembered the party atmosphere, with food and wine stalls and the competing calls of the vendors. *The Temple has turned into just such a show,* he thought with sorrow.

But he had to move on with his day. Perplexed by the absence of priests and Temple personnel, Isaac decided to investigate. He stepped into the inner Temple, where there were seats for the richest of the faithful, but he found only the warm smell of recently lit incense. As he turned and headed for the men's court, he saw a young scribe—new to the Temple—scurrying through the hallway connecting the courts.

Isaac hailed him and grabbed his arm. "Where is everyone?" he asked with some concern. "Is something going on this morning that I don't know about?"

The young scribe's hair was tussled, and there was a cut on his left hand. He burst forth in excited anger, "There's a madman in the Temple! In the Court of the Gentles!"

Isaac let go of the boy and stepped back. "You mean like the demon-possessed man who was here a couple years ago?"

"That was before my time," the scribe said, in a rush to be off. "But this man might be possessed. I don't know! He's out there, overturning tables and whipping vendors, and animals are flying all over the place! It's a madhouse!"

Surely he's exaggerating, Isaac thought. But the vacant, empty feeling of the Temple belied his attempt at calm rationality. He'd known something was wrong from the moment he stepped in the door. As Isaac hurried along the passageway, faint sounds began to grow louder: hoofs rapping against the Temple stones, the shouts—angry ones?—of excited men, a woman's high-pitched scream.

What in the world is going on?

Pushing his way the last couple of paces, Isaac stood at the top of the Court of the Gentiles, where it met the Temple doors, and peered out onto chaos.

The young scribe had not been exaggerating after all. Vendors were quickly pulling their wares from their tables and stuffing them into bags. Animals scurried in terror as they sought a way out of the courtyard. A knot of people stood, transfixed, as they watched a man stride purposefully across the square, a small whip in his left hand.

As Isaac watched the scene unfold, the man came to one of the money changer's stalls—complete with a scale and charts showing the exchange rates in various currencies. After uttering a few words Isaac could not hear, the man pushed the table over backwards into the lap of the old man in charge of it. Cries of protest and anger rang out from the money changer and his wife, who cowered behind her husband. But the young man raised his hand and cracked the whip against the side of the stall in obvious frustration and anger. Isaac heard his voice resonate clearly across the courtyard.

"This is supposed to be a house of prayer!" he cried—more a sob, really.

"This ... "

The whip cracked.

"Is. Supposed ... "

Another flailing strike against the side of the table.

"To. Be ... "

The man whirled, the strands of the whip curling around him.

"A HOUSE OF PRAYER!" he bellowed, pointing the whip at the money changer. Then he circled around with the whip straight out in front of him, accusing everyone.

"And you have made it a house of robbers!" Sorrow, anger, and exasperation all mingled in the vigorous thrust of his voice. "*A house of robbers,*" he uttered more quietly, his shoulders suddenly slumping, as if he had spent all his energy in his outburst.

The onlookers, who had been frozen like Greek statues, began to come to life. A muttering undercurrent shook the crowd. Some were angry their stalls had been ransacked. Others seemed fearful this madman would come after them again. But none dared approach him. They began slowly moving away from him, while the man continued to stand in the courtyard. It was as if a spell had been broken, and the man was wondering if he had indeed created the mess around him.

Isaac looked into the crowd to find the priests—surely someone would escort this man out of the Temple's precincts? He caught a glimpse of several of the older scribes and priests huddled into a corner, conversing among themselves while throwing veiled glances at the man. Isaac could tell exactly what they were thinking:

Should we confront him? Maybe we should just ignore him and he'll go away?

How can we control the damage he's already done—it's the Passover and everyone will be talking about this chaos!

For a moment, Isaac considered turning and going back into the Temple, pretending he had not just witnessed the passionate outburst. It would surely be simpler, but this man appeared to be in pain—physically, emotionally, mentally. And as much as Isaac did not want to admit it to himself, the man had touched a nerve that ran deep inside him. He, too, was sickened by the desecration of the Temple. He, too, thought of the whole circus as a den of thieves.

Isaac started toward the younger man, who remained rooted to the spot, head bowed, lips moving. When Isaac reached him, he hesitated before stretching out his hand and tentatively touching the other man's elbow. When he did, the younger man flinched as if burned and jerked around, as if challenging Isaac. When he saw it was only a scribe, he took a step back and let the whip fall limply from his hands.

Isaac did not know what to say. Nothing in his training had prepared him to deal with crazy men overturning tables in the Temple courtyard. But he knew he couldn't leave this soul in distress. Turning his back on this man would sear his heart forever.

The younger man's eyes had not left Isaac's face. For the first time, Isaac looked at him carefully. His robe was muddied around the hem, and there was definitely the smell and smudge of animal dung on his right sleeve. The man was sweating—Isaac could smell it, raw and acrid—the exertion of his rampage taking its toll.

But the man's eyes and the tone of his skin tickled some long-forgotten memory. That strange, cinnamon-colored skin that appeared more often in Egyptians than Israelites. And those eyes ... shifting from brown to gold to hazel. Eyes full of compassion. Isaac wondered why this man would have compassion for *him*—surely it should be the other way around? Yet he felt as if this strange man looked into his soul and knew what he was thinking.

The man reached out and touched his sleeve. "You are Isaac," he said softly.

Now it was Isaac's turn to recoil, to yank his arm back from the stranger. No—surely it wasn't him. All the built-up dreams Isaac had had about this boy, how he was destined for greatness and how he wanted his own child to be like him—no, surely that unusual, wonderful child in the Temple twenty years ago hadn't grown up to become…this? A madman vandalizing the most sacred place in their faith? It couldn't be.

Isaac choked, his words coming out of lips so dry it felt like someone had stuffed sackcloth in his mouth. "You…you can't be…"

He stopped and gazed into the younger man's eyes, which gleamed with a wry smile.

"Yeshua?" he prompted. "Yes, it is I." He laughed softly. "But today I'm afraid I haven't come to help you find a gold ring, only to make a mess and keep people talking for a while."

Isaac knew he must look mentally incompetent, with his mouth hanging open and face slack and white. Yeshua watched him for a moment, then laughed again. "Is it really so strange to see me here?" he asked. "Didn't I once say I needed to be in my Father's house?"

Isaac cleared his throat and swallowed hard. "I can't believe it's really you," he said slowly, examining Yeshua's face again. "I have thought of you often over the years. I have wondered how you fared."

Yeshua raised both hands and shrugged his shoulders. "This probably isn't what you envisioned, right?" He chuckled. Around him, the vendors continued cleaning up the mess, and Isaac wondered how long it would be before the Temple guards grabbed Yeshua and dragged him out of the building— or demanded he pay back what he'd damaged.

Isaac put his arm around Yeshua's shoulder, looking about covertly. "Come along with me and we'll talk," he said. "Let's get you out of here."

Yeshua followed Isaac across the courtyard, along the shortest route that would take them away from the once again hectic and bustling crowds. With pilgrims constantly filling the courtyard square, several hundred new people had crowded in since the incident, unaware of what had happened. Isaac deliberately melted into the crowd as they headed in the direction of a small, seldom-used storage room.

Walking ahead of the tired young man, whose shoulders slumped and who seemed to follow Isaac as obediently as a dog in the street, Isaac kept pushing through the crowds, using his elbows and knees to clear a path. They sidled past a turbaned man with several missing teeth, who stank of garlic; they bumped headlong into a young man trying to catch a lamb that had broken free from his makeshift pen. Finally, they stepped over the wooden threshold into a terrace that housed old potted palms and benches—a cool refuge for the priests who had time on their hands during the day. Isaac slowed down, making sure they were alone. He waited for Yeshua to catch up with him, then proceeded to a small door on the eastern side of the Temple.

He lifted the latch and pushed with both palms, the door protesting with the whine of seldom-used hinges. Stepping into a dim hallway that smelled musty and cold, Isaac motioned for Yeshua to follow him into the first room on the left. The Temple's extra candlesticks and incense were stored here, along with broken seats, a once richly colored tapestry that was now faded and worn, and ceremonial trumpets used for the festivals of Sukkot and Purim.

Finding nothing better to sit on than a rust-colored pillow with stuffing pouring out the side seam, Isaac motioned Yeshua onto it while he gingerly seated himself on a chair with a broken back.

"A lot of junk in here," Isaac said, looking around with a rueful smile. "But if I asked whose responsibility it is to clean it out, I'm afraid I'd know the answer. Probably better to leave well enough alone."

Yeshua had not said a word since leaving the cramped and chaotic Court of the Gentiles. He appeared in no hurry to fill the conversational void, and Isaac began to feel uneasy. What, exactly, was he supposed to say to someone he had not seen in twenty years—and then only briefly, in a quick adventure that had been forgotten by everyone in the Temple except him? But Yeshua remembered the ring, too. He remembered meeting Isaac.

Yeshua lifted his hands as if about to say something, then let them fall back into his lap. "I probably owe you some sort of explanation for what happened out there," he began, glancing at Isaac to see if he expected one. But Isaac had shrugged his shoulders as if to say, "It's your business, not mine."

Yeshua looked back down, and his attention was caught by the worn tapestry at his side. Although it was folded into a square the size of a blanket, it was obviously a very large piece of fabric. He reached out and caressed it.

Isaac cleared his throat and tried to make small talk. "That's a very fine curtain," he said. "We used it for many years as the inner veil, but it became shabby. The weather, you know—the lack of humidity makes the fibers come loose after a while ... "

He trailed off lamely. As if Yeshua wanted to talk about tapestries.

But Yeshua continued to finger the cloth thoughtfully. He looked up and asked suddenly, "What do you use now?"

Isaac was taken aback. What *did* they use now? He had to think a moment. "Well, last year the merchant, Eliazer— he lives on the western side of the city and sells dyes—he donated a new tapestry. It's quite beautiful ... has designs of angels and winged creatures on it. If you'd like ... to see it?"

Yeshua didn't speak for a moment, just stared down at his lap. "It's unbearable," he said quietly. "It's all *unbearable*."

Isaac felt a stab of compassion for the troubled young man. "I know," he said quietly. "I've had the same thoughts. The Court of the Gentiles is a disgrace ... "

Yeshua cut him off with a flick of his hand. "That's not it," he said hoarsely, then stopped. "Well, that's not *all* of it."

He stopped again, as if the words were being wrung from him. Slowly. Painfully. He started again.

"To see people reaching out to the Father, then being treated like refuse, like second-hand garments that aren't worth anything." He motioned to the curtain at his side. "To see the people of God being held back from Him by a curtain—how has Israel come to this?"

Isaac was shocked to hear a man he supposed to be a devout Jew speak like this. "But it's the Law of Elohim," he whispered. "Surely you know the people cannot come to Him alone. They must go through the priest. They must go through the Temple. It's the only way." He leaned forward, breathless, insistent, trying to convince this young man of the rightness of his argument.

Yeshua's hand covered his mouth, and he moved it in agitation across his lips. "No more," he muttered. "No more. There is so much to do this week and so little time. Father, make me strong. Father, hold me up."

Isaac reached out and rested his long, white fingertips on Yeshua's bronzed wrist. He finally understood. The exhaustion of travel, combined with the crowds and heat, had slightly unhinged Yeshua.

"Have you come from far away?" he asked, his voice solicitous. "I understand how the Passover week affects everyone—there are only so many hours in the day to sacrifice and pray and visit the Temple. We're half-mad with the crowds and the noise and the work."

Yeshua looked up as if he had forgotten Isaac was there. "This is a very hard week for me," he continued in a monotone that made Isaac wonder if this strange young man knew where he was or to whom he was talking. Yeshua's eyes were focused over Isaac's head, and his voice was low and insistent. Isaac withdrew his touch and said nothing, simply let Yeshua finish his murmuring—was he praying?

Then came a half minute of silence, with only dust motes floating in the stream of light coming through the tiny rectangular window near the ceiling. Yeshua's eyes flicked down and met Isaac's. His voice now seemed ordinary and warm.

"Thank you for your kindness," he said. "Thank you for your understanding."

Isaac rose from his broken chair. He really needed to make sure it was thrown out. He towered above Yeshua, still seated on the ground, not really sure what to say to him.

"I—I really haven't done anything," he finally answered. "I think you need a bit of a rest and maybe some time to pray … ?"

Yeshua rose rather awkwardly from the overstuffed pillow and clasped Isaac's hands in his. "I am praying constantly this week," he said earnestly, looking straight down into Isaac's face. Isaac was tall, but now he had to look up to see Yeshua's eyes. "And I will pray for you and your family and for the students you seek."

Isaac stared wordlessly at Yeshua and instinctively pulled his hands away. Who *was* this strange young man? How did he know Isaac was seeking more students—he hadn't even told his own wife yet, let alone anyone at the Temple! What was wrong with him? Could he be demon-possessed? After all, those who were filled with demons were said to be able to tell the future.

Isaac backed away slowly. He needed time to think, to make sense of everything. It was all too … supernatural. Musing about this boy today on the way to the Temple. Running into him again in most peculiar circumstances. Having this bizarre conversation. He just wanted … Yeshua gone.

As if once again reading Isaac's mind, the younger man pushed a lock of hair out of his eyes and turned to the door. Isaac wanted to ask him where he would go but realized he really didn't want to know. Yeshua reached the door frame while Isaac continued to stand frozen, staring after him.

One hand on the lintel, Yeshua half-turned and looked at Isaac again. In the faraway distance of time and space—as if the outer market were a world far beyond the stars—Isaac could faintly hear the bleat of a goat and the angry imprecations of two men. Had he been part of that world only a few minutes ago? How long had it been since he'd seen this calm young man acting like a maniac in the Temple?

"Blessed are you, Isaac ben Rahim," Yeshua intoned as if he were speaking a Sabbath invocation. "Blessed are those who seek, even when they're not sure what they're seeking."

Yeshua gave a barely discernible parting smile, turned, and walked out the door. Isaac could hear his sandaled footsteps vanishing down the hallway. Then, once again, the high whine of the outside door before it shuddered into place.

Isaac felt a chill run down his spine. Suddenly, he longed for the noise and smell of the Temple courtyards. The dizzying heat of the white-hot day. The droning cry of the peddlers. Suddenly ... he longed for what he knew.

- RUCHEL -

Roasted lamb. That thought kept Ruchel going during this week of unending food preparations and herb-crusted dishes to wash. A week of extra visitors for the Passover, with all the attendant duties—airing musty, unused bedrooms; polishing the intricately detailed flooring in the entry hall; preparing special meals for visitors with delicate stomachs, like the old scribe who couldn't tolerate garlic and needed to have all his food bland and unflavored.

But the lamb—Ruchel thought of the succulent, dripping meat through the hours of drudgery and moments when she was so exhausted she would have gladly dropped onto the pile of linens she was hauling to the laundry. In a poor family, lamb was a treat only tasted at Passover, and even then there had been years when her family substituted a less expensive wild goat, as did many of their neighbors. But this year—this year, they would have lamb, purchased from Zakor, the butcher. A lamb without spot or blemish, as required by Law.

Ruchel lifted her chin with pride, and she gave a small sniff. It was her earnings—yes, her doing—that had brought lamb into her family's household this year. Her service to her master would bring many good things to them.

Of course, there would be lamb in abundance at her master's household too, and it infuriated her that the left-overs would be burned before the evening was over. The thought of wasting so much savory meat made her slightly ill, but the Law required that no lamb remain by morning. *It could be sent home with the servants*, Ruchel thought angrily. But of course her master took Moses' Law very literally—if servants could not partake in the Passover at his table, surely they couldn't be given any leftover lamb to take home to their hungry families, even if it were minced and added to lentils for stew.

Ruchel left her home and hurried along the cobblestone streets. Frost still lingered before sunrise in the month of Nisan. The stones were uneven and would have punctured her feet if they weren't so hardened. But every poor child in Palestine had tough, leather-like feet, the result of their mothers working oil into them from the moment they were born, a practicality that made shoes unnecessary most of the year.

"A pity, since she has such beautiful feet," her mother had reportedly said when the aunts began the olive oil regimen at her birth, massaging it systematically into Ruchel's heels and instep. In the end, her mother could not afford such sentimentality. Only the daughters of wealthy families—the scribes, the Pharisees, the estate managers—could boast soft, white feet at their marriages. From the moment Ruchel was born, her mother knew she would have to be put into service at an early age.

But oh … they had never dreamed of how far she would go! To be a helper in an herb stall, yes, or to work for a wealthy mother with many children, certainly. But to be offered a position with Caiaphas—even now, her mother could barely speak of it! To be chosen to work in the household of the high priest—it was something not to be fathomed or understood. Only by the grace of Yahweh had it been made possible.

Ruchel smirked a little at her mother's naïve wonder. After working for Caiaphas for more than a year, she wasn't so sure the Almighty had that much to do with it. It was more likely her pure bloodlines had secured her place. Caiaphas wanted only the purest of the pure cleaning his private toilet and brushing the dust from his sandals. He would tolerate only those who could prove their genealogy was unsullied and without blemish—even in the most mundane positions in his household.

Ruchel remembered the frenzied procedure her father had gone through—her father, whose every thought and action was slow and measured—to prove his daughter's heritage when he'd first been approached by the rabbi of the synagogue.

An opening for a servant girl in Caiaphas' household! Hurry, man, put her pedigree together and get her in there. This will open doors unknown to any of us!

No doubt the rabbi had thought even the impoverished synagogues of such servants could benefit by way of the few extra coins given at holidays by rich masters in their servants' names.

And so her father had pulled out the broken bits of papyrus that detailed their family line. As required, he outlined the past seven generations of Ruchel's family. No Gentiles. No one who had committed a crime, though the fact that Great-Grandfather Ezekiel had once been accused of stealing a donkey caused a few moments' worry for her father. No one born illegitimate (what a shame that would be!). No one dishonoring the family name or casting doubt on the last seven generations of the house of Ruchel's father and mother, both of the tribe of Benjamin.

Pedigree in hand, the rabbi had approached Caiaphas' assistant and asked for a place in the household for Ruchel. His case was persuasive: She was eleven, hard-working, the oldest daughter of many children, and well-versed in the ways of a household. Most important, she was of pure stock. When word came later that day that she would be taken on for a probation period of three moons, the entire family exulted. Ruchel was sent out to buy pomegranates— *pomegranates*—at great cost for the celebration.

Nearly a year later, Ruchel still believed in her good fortune, though the glamour—neighbors stopping her in the street with *mazel tovs*, the rabbi pronouncing a special blessing at the synagogue—had worn off. The work was hard, so hard that most nights Ruchel returned home and collapsed in a death-like sleep. Her hands had become as hardened as her feet, mostly from the scrubbing salts used to clean the floors and dishes, brought a great distance from the mines near the Dead Sea. And Caiaphas was a stingy bastard. Though he seldom deigned to enter the kitchen or laundry, he had a network of assistants and spies who reported all that went on. It was difficult to smuggle out even a couple of figs or the remnants of a barley stew, which would be thrown out anyway. Those in Caiaphas' employ learned craftiness early.

But there were benefits. All those in the upper echelon of Caiaphas' vast circle of employ—his personal scribes, his property overseers, his housekeeper—lived in a complex on his property. The backs of their small, separate residences opened onto a large courtyard. Early in the morning, before official duties called, all the servants met to talk and warm themselves there around a large fire.

Gossiped, more like it. They chattered of who was preparing what for Sukkot and Rosh Hashanah. They spoke of who was already expecting so soon after their wedding. They tut-tutted over the behavior of the third scribe's son, who had spoken rudely to the housekeeper the day before and was making a name for himself as a *havach*—a disrespectful boy. And they marveled over visitors from different provinces around the country who brought unheard-of delights—strange fruits, fabrics unknown around Jerusalem, news of a far-away emperor's doings.

And, of course, there were the romances, the matchmaking, the betrothals that took place among Caiaphas' extended network of employees. Ruchel's mother prayed her daughter would make a good match among the boys she worked with—perhaps they'd stay on together and live in the compound. They would be set for life! It was her most ardent wish that Adonai would, in His mercy, send a suitable husband for her Ruchel. If not, there was that cousin, Elkanah, who would suffice. But Ruchel could do so much better than a donkey seller's son!

Ruchel had had her share of attention, but it wasn't the kind she wanted her mother to know about. Ruchel knew she was not beautiful. Her mouth was too large, and her developing hips too narrow. She had inherited her father's small, wiry build, and she knew men preferred the soft roundness of Abigail, the new laundry maid. But Ruchel's unusual honey-brown hair—a throwback to her great-great-grandmother—was always beautifully brushed and swept up in an elaborate bun that kept it out of the food and fire. And her voice! Ruchel's aunts had always said she could charm the birds out of the trees when she sang, and she often sang as she went about her work.

A few months after beginning her employment, Ruchel had found herself alone one morning in the rinse laundry. The gardener's son—a sniveling, pimply fourteen-year-old—backed her against the wall and stuck his hand down the front of her tunic, roughly pinching her breasts.

Ruchel was no innocent. As the oldest of eight children, knowledge of what happened between a man and a woman had come early. So she kicked the boy in the shins, leaving him sniffling and whining about just having fun.

"Next time, I'll kick you a little higher," Ruchel promised, and the boy slunk away.

After that, Ruchel noticed the servant girls of the household always worked in pairs, and she fell into the practice. As her mother often commented, a poor girl had little to bring to her marriage other than her virtue. And Ruchel had heard the whispers about the unfortunate girl in the head steward's household who had been "taken advantage of," then sent home in disgrace when she'd turned up expecting. She did not intend for that sort of thing to happen to her or her family. Her three *denarii* a week—and more importantly, the honor of having a job in Caiaphas' household, no matter how menial—kept her family's head up with pride.

At other times, the courtyard was a place of mocking and gibing. That was when the poor unfortunates that Caiaphas' spies hauled in for questioning were tormented in full sight of all the households. Breaking Sabbath laws, not paying Temple tax—those were the ordinary, run-of-the-mill offenses that at best provided a break in the day and at worst were degrading and painful to watch. Many of the servants had hung their heads in shame as their own relatives were so derided.

Caiaphas' underlings put the condemned through their paces, twisting their words until the offenders simply gave up and agreed to do whatever was asked of them.

Yes, kind sir, I'll go back home and no longer allow my child to kick a ball in the streets on the Sabbath—until three stars have appeared in the sky to proclaim the Sabbath over.

Yes, good master, I'll pay the Temple tax, even though it means I'll not be able to feed my family next week.

Caiaphas himself rarely appeared at these exhibitions and almost never allowed them in his great hall. They were simply beneath him, and he let his minions do his work, just as he gave Ruchel the privilege of washing his underwear in the great stone laundry basins.

Yesterday, another of these poor fellows had been summoned before Caiaphas—but all the circumstances of his arrest had been unusual. The entire Council had been called to convene quickly in the great hall, and Ruchel had laughed as one of the chief scribes showed up with his napkin still tucked into his tunic, evidently having been plucked straight from his dinner table. The unfortunate man was brought in chains and—most unusual—trailed by a large band of disciples who then loitered at the gate to the courtyard. Eventually, they warily crept up to the fire to warm themselves.

It wasn't that having a band of followers was so strange. Many rabbis hand-picked their adherents, who hung on their every word, taking notes, and asking questions. But what was so bewildering were the kind of men and boys following this teacher. Even Ruchel, with her limited schooling, knew these men to be rough and uncultured, so unlike the pale scholastics who devoted their lives to following other teachers.

These were men of the outdoors. As one of them reached out for a piece of bread at the fire, Ruchel could see his forearms were scarred with what appeared to be rope burns. Their skin was swarthy and wind burnt.

Ruchel contrasted them to Uncle Isaac, who sat in the Temple as a follower of the great Rabbi Koletz. Isaac had rarely set foot outside as a student, as he dug deeply into the Scriptures and sat at the Temple doors with his teacher, discussing the holy texts eight to ten hours a day. To earn his living, he worked as a scribe at the Temple and taught the Torah to young boys, as well as basic reading, writing, and mathematics. Isaac was pale, almost anemic-looking, as befit any good disciple who spent his life studying. What kind of rabbi would want this darkened, weather-hardened riffraff following him, with their strange, coarse clothing? Their appearance all but proclaimed they had no time to hang on a rabbi's words. And their accent was strange—the way they rolled their *r's*, the nasal sound of the *ch*. Ruchel had never heard anything like it before and asked the chief housemaid about it.

"They sound like the Galilean fishermen who sometimes sell at the market," she said. "It's really too far for them, but when they have an unusually large catch, they'll set up here."

They all seemed incredibly exotic—albeit a little frightening—to Ruchel. While she wanted to know more about them and their strange teacher, she was taken aback by their unkempt hair and bold, staring eyes. The chief housemaid continued.

"See those burns? These are fishermen—those marks are from the nets pulling across their arms when they have a large catch."

Ruchel had left late last evening—too much work, too many things to finish up, the strange disciples—and now she was returning well before dawn.

I should have found a place in a corner to sleep, she thought, though her mother would have worried when she didn't return home. She wondered absently about the man who had appeared before the Council last night, whose proceedings were still going on when she left.

Yeshua, someone said his name was. *From Galilee. Strange man, doing all kinds of things to irk the Council.* But surely his crimes must be more than a Sabbath violation? Ruchel had never seen anyone brought before Caiaphas in chains for that. He must have committed some terrible infraction against the synagogue or the Council or … surely not … against Elohim— the Creator God—Himself.

Ruchel gasped with the enormity of that possibility. She and her mother had once come upon a stoning outside the marketplace, on their way home from choosing cloth for winter dresses. Ruchel had been too small to understand what was happening, but when her mother had seen the upraised arms with rocks—some of them practically boulders—and heard the mocking cries of the crowd, she'd grabbed Ruchel harshly by the shoulders and spun her around, dragging her back the way they had come.

Surely this man—this Yeshua—would not be stoned?

He appeared to be a plain man, from the quick glimpses Ruchel got of him. Clean-shaven, dark brown hair, a wind- burnt face like the rest of his disciples—what *were* they doing outdoors? What kind of teacher was he? There was talk among the other servants that this man had done brave and exciting things in the countryside surrounding Jerusalem, but that didn't really matter to Ruchel. Her year had been so full, so consuming as she learned the rituals of Caiaphas' household. She didn't have time to spare for an itinerant wanderer who supposedly made miracles. Other teachers had done these things too and been proven frauds. Of greater interest to her were his followers—their crude, uncouth ways and how they mixed with Caiaphas' servants like olive oil and vinegar.

It certainly made for an exciting diversion in a week full of the unusual. Ruchel would watch. She would wait. She would, in her mother's words, "keep her mouth shut and her ears open."

Something told her it would be an unsettling day.

- ELKANAH -

Elkanah still stood, stunned, his mind a muddle of feelings and excuses and protests. He grabbed his stomach and reeled over, as if he had been kicked in the gut by a donkey. His breath came in short gasps, and when he tried to stand up, his head spun. Just as he thought he would pass out in a heap on the cobbled stones of the courtyard, a surge of pure anger forced him upright.

Something had been taken that was *his*. He didn't have much in this life, but Sha-Khohr was *his*. The colt had been given into his care. He was Elkanah's to tend and protect. And he had failed to do that. And by Hashem, he would get Sha-Khohr back.

Elkanah stopped to breathe a minute, pulling air into his straining lungs, considering his situation. The men who had taken the colt were a good ten minutes ahead of him, and they were headed down the hill, into Bethphage. Without changing out of his dirt-caked sandals or sweaty tunic, Elkanah charged ahead, looking for the bleached muslin garb of the strange men who had stolen his colt.

As he crested the summit of the hill and began the descent into the village, he considered his options. Who exactly was he going to complain to? One didn't get the Romans involved in these kinds of issues. The less they were around, the better. The Temple police didn't have the authority to deal with problems outside the Temple grounds. And, he had to admit, the men who'd taken Sha-Khohr hadn't seemed violent or threatening; in fact, they'd seemed as bewildered as Elkanah, as if they weren't sure why they were taking the colt in the first place.

Still, a plan formed in his mind. Elkanah would find the men, find Sha-Khohr, and follow them. He'd make sure they weren't mistreating the colt and take the animal back as soon as he could.

Then a troubling thought struck him: If they were taking Sha-Khohr into Jerusalem, he would definitely lose them. It was only a little over a mile away, but the streets were already crowded for the upcoming Passover festival, when the city swelled by hundreds of thousands of people. If he didn't catch up with them now, he might lose Sha-Khohr forever.

Elkanah's pace quickened and he stumbled, stopping to dig a pebble out of his sandal. A neighbor called to him in greeting, but Elkanah didn't hear. He plunged into the heart of Bethphage, eyes straining for the sight of two men with a black colt. *They couldn't be walking that quickly*, he thought, *not with a colt.* He should have found them by now. By the time Elkanah entered the eastern gate of the village, he was breathing hard and needed to stop a moment.

Use your head, he thought. *For once, don't panic—think it through.* It suddenly occurred to him that he wasn't afraid. He wasn't afraid of what his father would say. He wasn't afraid of the men who'd taken Sha-Khohr. He wasn't even afraid they would mistreat the donkey.

How do you know that? an inner voice jeered. *You might never see him again.*

But for once, Elkanah stifled the niggling self-doubt, and he knew something was about to happen, something that would change him.

People rushed past him toward the middle of town. Bethphage's proximity to Jerusalem meant all the inns would be full, but even for Passover week, it was unusual for the village to be this crowded this early. They all seemed to know where they were going, so Elkanah reached out and touched an older man whose hair and beard were grizzled and white.

"What's happening?" Elkanah gestured toward the crowd. "It's not a market today, is it?"

The old man peered up at Elkanah with rheumy eyes, as if trying to find where the voice was coming from. He wheezed slightly with the exertion of trying to keep up. "Everyone's talking about some man who claims to be the Messiah," the old man gasped. "He's going to parade into Jerusalem from Bethphage!"

That's all I need right now. Elkanah sighed. These kinds of parades happened sometimes, bringing out the bored and morbidly curious who wanted to see how the Romans would handle it. Though they all knew where it would end: a ghastly, slow death on a cross. But that awful fate didn't seem to deter those who had hopes of unseating the Romans—the earnest and the zealous who had plans and maps and weapons and a following; the rich who worked behind the scenes, funding rebels but never getting their own hands dirty; the crazy who, having been pushed too far by taxes and heavy fines, suddenly brandished weapons and shouted threats.

Well, the two men and his colt would be caught up in the same crowd, so they wouldn't be able to get too far ahead. Elkanah pushed himself through the stream of humanity, past women who had stopped to look at the wares on sale at a pot vendor, past children throwing a ball into the air who stopped in terror when that ball hit the side of an older man's head. Elkanah laughed, remembering when he and Bashel had done the same thing, hoping to escape with their ball before the offended party began to chase them or—worse yet—find their father.

It had to be close to midday. As he pushed into the market square, Elkanah regretted that it *wasn't* a market day—he was hungry and would have loved biting into some juicy figs from the countryside. He'd started toward the well in the center of the plaza, anticipating the tang of icy water from its depths, when he caught a glimpse of black fur in the shifting mass of people. He couldn't see who was walking alongside the animal—had he found Sha-Khohr?

He pressed ahead, keeping his eyes glued to the spot of obsidian. Now that Elkanah had spotted Sha-Khohr, he wondered again what possible use a colt with a damaged hoof could be to two strangers. If they had stolen him with a view to selling, this was the wrong day. To haul a load? If that were the case, why didn't the strangers take a larger, older donkey? Elkanah remembered their words.

"After we're through with him, we'll get someone to take him back."

Even they had seemed unsure why they needed Sha-Khohr.

Elkanah realized the spot of black had stopped and materialized into his little colt. He stood about twenty feet away, trying to peer through the crowd. Sha-Khohr looked scared, but he wasn't fighting the halter or throwing his head from side to side, as he usually did when agitated. An arrow of love and compassion and anger shot through Elkanah. What could these men possibly be doing?

He could see the Galileans clearly now. They weren't moving—they were standing there, holding the colt's lead rope, looking around, as if they were waiting for someone. *This is ridiculous*, Elkanah thought. *I should just go up there, take the rope out of their hands, and leave.* But curiosity had taken over. Now that he knew Sha-Khohr was all right, he truly wanted to see what would happen next.

The two men seemed to be arguing, one of them waving his arms with the rope in hand. The man not holding the rope was placating his friend, trying to calm him down. He placed a soothing hand on the angry man's arm. Whatever was going on, these men were anxious.

As he began to inch forward, Elkanah felt a touch on his arm. Aware that pickpockets hung around the plaza, he whirled around. A grown man gazed down at him with a questioning look. As Elkanah stared, he felt he had seen this man before. His eyes … they were most unusual. Not brown, not green, with flecks of hazel. The boy realized he was standing mutely, as if he were mentally deficient.

"Yes?" Elkanah ventured, wondering if the man had meant to get someone else's attention, but there was no one close to them.

"You seem to be focused on that little donkey," the man said. "Is it for sale?"

Elkanah took a deep breath, feeling as if a dam had burst inside his chest.

"It's *my* donkey!" he exclaimed. "Those men came to my father's business and took him! They said they would bring him back later, but he's never had a rider, and he's lame! I followed them to be sure he wasn't being mistreated … "

The man looked from the boy to the donkey, still being held by the two men who had by now noticed his arrival.

"Perhaps their master had need of him," the stranger said gently to Elkanah.

Elkanah's eyes grew wide and his jaw dropped. "That's *exactly* what they said!" he blurted. "How did you know that? And who is their master?"

The man grasped Elkanah's shoulder and squeezed it. He said gently, "Your little donkey will be returned to you, safe and whole." Then he walked toward the two men and talked with them briefly. The larger of the two helped the man mount Sha-Khohr, and the other led the donkey with its rider away from the plaza. The man's feet touched the ground—he was almost too large for the little beast.

Elkanah stood, frozen. *He* was the master? Then the old man's words came back to him.

The Messiah? Parading into Jerusalem?

A wave of panic overtook him. He didn't want this man coming to a bad end because he claimed to be the Messiah. He didn't want the two men with him to be hurt. And he didn't want his donkey in the procession. What if the Romans arrested the man and his followers and took Sha-Khohr?

The man's words rang in his ears. *"Your little donkey will be returned to you, safe and whole."*

How could he know? Yet the look in the man's eyes had reassured Elkanah. What should he do now?

He couldn't follow the procession into Jerusalem. His father would beat him for leaving the stables for the entire day. And the thought of getting tangled up with the Romans made him ill.

Elkanah turned, took a breath, and made a decision. He would trust this man and his strange disciples, even though every fiber of his being cried out against it.

Reluctantly, Elkanah started back toward home.

- RUCHEL -

The time just after breakfast preparations, but before the day's activities truly began, was a favorite for all Caiaphas' servants. Ruchel breathed deeply as she stood in the courtyard. The sun was not up yet, and she could see the mist of her breath wafting on the air. She treasured these moments out of the claustrophobic warmth of the kitchen. With its massive fires and cloying odors of cooking onions and horseradish, the great heart of the house could quickly sicken anyone who worked there too long.

Not much seemed to have happened with the strange group of men who'd been hanging about the estate when she'd left last night. At least, that's what she surmised from the housemaids who had stayed overnight and the young groundskeeper's wife, who joined her at the fire in the courtyard.

"They all sort of ... drifted off," the woman said, seeming rather disappointed by the anticlimax.

"And the Yeshua one?" Ruchel asked, rather disinterestedly. "Is he gone, too?"

"*No.*" Ruchel looked up quickly at the other woman's firm tone. "*He* has not been seen since he was taken inside—and neither have any of the Council members who were summoned to meet him."

An ominous silence fell. Both women knew that whatever this Yeshua had done, it was not a good sign if he was still inside. Ruchel asked the question she had been wondering all night.

"But what did he *do*? What is he accused of?"

The groundskeeper's wife pulled her shawl tighter around her head and looked over her shoulder, obviously wanting to keep the conversation for Ruchel's ears only. Ruchel stepped in toward her, realizing this situation must be serious.

The woman ran her tongue across her lips and looked uneasy. For several seconds, she said nothing, then stammered, "I-I'm only repeating what I've heard from Jacov, the stable boy, and of course from my husband ... "

She stopped, as if debating whether to share something of such magnitude. "I've heard ... anyway, people are saying ... Yeshua claims to be the *Mashiach* ... the Messiah."

Ruchel jerked away as if the woman had just thrust a snake into her hands. It was unbelievable ... inconceivable! To claim something so outrageous was more than just lunacy—it was heresy! It meant death both spiritually and physically for anyone bold enough—or deranged enough—to utter the words.

The groundskeeper's wife shook her head. "And it's been said that he has been silent before the Council ... absolutely silent." Her voice became excited, warming to the gossip. "All sorts of accusations have been made against him, and he says *nothing*."

A thought struck Ruchel. "Perhaps," she began. "Perhaps it's a misunderstanding. People just thought they heard him say that ... you know how stories get started!"

The groundskeeper's wife shook her head again, this time sadly. *What is her name again?* Ruchel wondered. *Devorah? Devana?*

"Too many people have heard it," she whispered. "For one thing, I've heard tell he stood up in his home synagogue and claimed to be the fulfillment of the book of the blessed prophet Isaiah. My father's aunt attends there, far away in Nazareth, and she said they about stoned him for it!"

A stab of pity filled Ruchel for this poor, misguided man. No one who made such outlandish claims could hope to stand against Caiaphas and his Council—let alone against the Roman authorities. It sickened her to think which of them would get him first. The Council could make things miserable for Yeshua, but when it came right down to it, they had no legal authority to punish someone. She remembered his plain, pleasant face as he'd been lead through the courtyard. In the pit of her stomach, she knew his end would not be a good one.

Ruchel remained at the fire for a few more minutes, wishing she had brought a cup of strong, sweet tea to warm her up. She ticked through the list of jobs she needed to finish today: airing the beds and tidying up the bedrooms; churning the last of the cream into the golden butter, a treat unknown in her own meager household; helping the cook with whatever tasks were put in front of her today.

With a sigh, Ruchel pulled her shawl tighter and turned away from the fire. *Time to get going,* she thought. As she moved toward the laundry, she caught someone standing on the edge of the courtyard in the corner of her eye. She peered through the semi-darkness ... yes, it was one of *them*! One of the followers of this Yeshua fellow. Evidently, he was waiting to see what became of his rabbi.

Ruchel's curiosity got the better of her. She knew she should walk on, not get involved. She knew a well-bred Jewish girl did not speak to strange men, even Jewish men, but too much had been said around the compound about this strange group; if she could talk with this man, she'd have some choice gossip to share.

Pulling her shawl up over her head, she approached the man, who shivered in the doorway, a rough linen coat pulled tight around him. "Why don't you come over to the fire?" Ruchel asked him, standing several feet away. "The morning is frosty."

Silence. The man looked miserable, and not just because of the cold. His eyes were bleary and red. His coat was dirty, and his hair was stiff with grime and dust. But it was the look of total desperation in his eyes, tinged with panic, that made him appear wild and untamed. Ruchel looked around to see who else was in the courtyard; she had surely made a mistake coming to talk to this crazy man. Seeing that a group of gardeners and dairymaids were still loitering around the fire, she found the courage to speak again.

"Are you here to see someone?" she pressed. "You can come over to the fire while you're waiting."

The man looked unsure whether to answer, then the words burst forth and he sputtered, "Yes, I'm waiting for someone."

Ah, he is *a Galilean*, Ruchel thought, hearing his distinctive northern accent. Well, she certainly intended to pump him for information, though tendrils of sympathy threaded their way through her mind. *He looks so bereft*, she thought, *so full of despair.*

Her tone softened a little. "Come. While you're waiting, you can warm yourself."

The man hesitated but finally gave in. He took a few tentative steps toward the fire, pulling his coat even tighter. Standing at the edge of the ring of charcoal embers, away from the others who still lingered, he stared into the flames, lost in thought.

Ruchel followed, standing next to him. She was proud of herself for coaxing this stranger to the fire and decided to show off a little in front of the others.

"You're waiting for the one they call Yeshua, then?" she asked innocently.

The man recoiled as if she had thrust a burning coal at him. "No, no, not at all. I don't know who that is. I'm—I'm waiting for someone else."

There was a burst of smothered laughter from the gardener on the other side of the fire. "You're a Galilean all right. We can hear it in your voice. You must be with that Yeshua lunatic."

The man's eyes flared with panic, mixed with anger. "I tell you, that's *not right*. I don't even *know* that man you're talking about!" He clenched his fist, as if he would march around the fire and swing at the gardener, but he checked himself.

"All right, all right," soothed the gardener, holding out his hands in a gesture of peace. "If you say you're not, who are we to question you? We just want to know what this Yeshua character has done that he was dragged in here in chains."

The stranger appeared to go berserk. Ruchel watched in horror as he lifted his fist to heaven and called down curses on himself, swearing he did not know the arrested man as he ripped his clothing and fell to his knees in front of the fire. She realized he was mad and probably dangerous, and she stepped away into the shadows of the men on other side of the fire.

Perhaps he's having a fit? Or maybe he's just lost his mind, she thought. *They will lock him up, him and his teacher.* She stared at him, amazed. Nothing like this had ever disrupted the tidy rituals of Caiaphas' household. Surely the guards would be here soon to take him away?

The man suddenly stopped cursing and raving. He seemed spent, and he bowed down in front of the fire, his head on his knees, taking rapid, shallow breaths. Everyone stood as if paralyzed, not knowing what to do. Should they help him up? Walk away? No one wanted to be associated with him, just as he did not want to be associated with the unfortunate man being interrogated. It was a terrible thing to behold, this man who was so eaten up with pain and rage.

As they stood—frozen as if they were in one of those tableau entertainments the Greeks performed in the market—the rooster across the courtyard crowed. The man's head jerked upward, as if he weren't sure what he had heard. It broke the spell, and as the servants around the fire looked at each other they knew the workday had truly begun. One by one, they drifted off to their stations, leaving Ruchel standing across the ring from the stranger, who had prostrated himself onto the chill, damp stones. His hands were behind his head, his tunic hiked up so a shocking amount of bare skin showed. But Ruchel could not avert her eyes. She watched as sobs heaved through his entire body, as he lay there broken by whatever was tormenting him.

Ruchel could not bear to watch and felt shame for the man. As she backed away from his writhing form, she could hear two words repeated over and over.

"Forgive me ... "

- Epilogue -

It had been almost three years since her gossip-inducing, disastrous wedding ceremony. The anniversaries of her marriage had largely gone unnoticed. It was as if she and Ezra had made a tacit agreement not to recall it.

But time does, indeed, heal wounds, as Shoshannah's mother had always said. Her heart no longer ached with yearning for a man she could not have; instead, a small sore spot was dedicated to the memory of the naïve, idealistic girl she had been. A fool in more ways than one.

As she took down the loaf of bread from the kitchen shelf for the evening meal, she had to admit her life had become quite pleasant. She was the mistress of her own home, even though it was only several rooms on the back of her in-laws' house. The nearness to her mother-in-law, Lilith, could be suffocating at times. But by and large, Lilith left her to her own devices and did not interfere in their lives. Shoshannah had noticed a tentative manner about Lilith, one that was curious about Shoshannah's secrets, from her strange betrothal to her chaotic wedding.

But Shoshannah would not share those secrets with Lilith—or even, in their entirety, with Ezra. He knew some of the story of her love affair with Nathaniel, but he had never plumbed the depths of her pain, just as she had only half-guessed about Ezra's lost love. They each had the right to hold some things to themselves.

As her wedding anniversary approached, Shoshannah again wondered about the dearth of wine and the seemingly impossible act Ezra's cousin, Yeshua, had performed—turning water into wine! A ridiculous proposition, but Shoshannah had examined it many times from one angle and another, and she could not come up with a more plausible explanation. Her husband seemed uninterested, saying simply, "Well, I'm glad my parents weren't shamed."

The rest of that evening played itself across her mind, including the conversation between Yeshua and his mother about his shabby clothing. Shoshannah had vowed that when she got her hands on a piece of quality fabric, she would make a tunic without seams for him—the gift of a distraught woman to a kind stranger.

And she had kept her promise. When Ezra's father had obtained a piece of lightweight wool in a rich, tawny brown and given it to his son, Shoshannah had known it was the piece of fabric she had been waiting for.

She'd carefully washed the cloth, which brought up the nap and prevented shrinking. She'd had to think hard to remember Yeshua's height, as she didn't usually sew something for someone without measuring them. He was, she recalled, much taller than Ezra, but not as broad through the shoulders. She would make the back a little longer than the front, to protect his body from the dew of the ground when he slept outdoors.

Even with all the guesswork, the tunic would have been serviceable as it was. But in a show of further appreciation, Shoshannah embroidered the hem with lilies—lilies in all the colors that bloomed in the Judean desert after the spring rains. Yeshua would remember that the lilies came from Shoshannah.

After months of work, the dilemma of how to get the tunic to Yeshua remained. He had not been seen in Cana since the wedding, though he seemed to drop in at Mary's home now and then.

"We never know when we're going to see him," Mary had told Lilith on a visit. "And then we never know if he'll be alone or with that whole horde!"

Lilith had decided a few months later to visit Mary for a week. Shoshannah had packed the tunic carefully, handing it to Lilith to deliver to her cousin. Lilith looked as if she were going to say something tart about giving a gift to a strange man, but when she saw Shoshannah's eyes, she bit her tongue. It was true, after all, that this itinerant had saved their reputation at the wedding. How he'd done it, Lilith didn't care. And so, she set off for Nazareth with the tunic on her lap.

When Lilith returned from Nazareth, she shared Mary's delight and laughter when she'd seen it was seamless.

"This is certainly the nicest thing he's had to wear for a long time!" Mary exclaimed. "And the lilies! This is really too beautiful for a wandering rabbi to wear!"

But she had given the tunic to Yeshua on his next visit, and he was touched by the gift—both by the practicality and the beauty.

Shoshannah shifted her mind back to the meal at hand, spooning up lentils into a bowl. Yes, life had treated her well, she decided. Ezra was dropping hints that he might begin building a separate home on the back of the property soon. His younger brother, Elimelech, was marrying next spring, and the new couple could move into Ezra and Shoshannah's lodgings. And, if Shoshannah was right, there was need for a larger home. She suspected that within seven months she would deliver a child. She hadn't told anyone yet, not even Ezra. For now, she hugged the secret to herself.

She realized she was looking forward to Ezra coming home that evening.

—

Elkanah jerked awake, knowing something had happened, but not remembering what. A feeling of dread hovered over him and suddenly crashed on his head: Sha-Khohr had been taken. He had been gone since yesterday morning, and Elkanah had not seen the colt since that fleeting glimpse in the market. The men—they had promised he would be returned unharmed, but when? And how could they make that promise with such certainty?

He pulled himself up from his mat, reluctant to dress, loath to face his family—his father—at the breakfast table. Joachim would want to know where the little donkey was and how his hoof was doing. There would be anger and shouting and disbelief that anyone's son could be so *stupid* as to let two strangers wander off with a piece of property.

Better to face his fate head on. Elkanah dragged himself down the steep ladder that separated the kitchen from the sleeping rooms and seated himself, waiting for his parents to sit down to begin the meal. His mother bustled around the kitchen, but there was no sign of Joachim. Elkanah began to sweat; surely his father had seen the empty stall, the missing beast. Surely he would come roaring into the kitchen any moment …

The door slammed outside in the courtyard, and Elkanah braced himself for the sight of his father, seething and pounding the furniture. But Joachim casually strode into the kitchen, whistling some tune, his voice downright jaunty.

"Whatever it is, it smells good!" he declared, nodding to his wife.

He must not have been to the barn yet this morning, Elkanah surmised. *Perhaps when breakfast is over and I go out to the barn, Sha-Khohr will be back.* He bent over his slice of flatbread, trying to avoid his father's eye.

"Well, I have to say, you did a good job on that little jack," Joachim boomed, beaming at Elkanah. "That foot looks like it never had any problem at all."

"What do you m-m-mean?" stammered Elkanah. "What about his foot?"

"Oh, come now," his father cajoled with a chuckle. "That salve you put on must have done the trick. And all that sunshine. You really spoiled that animal."

Elkanah choked down his bread as quickly as he could, ignoring his mother's offers of more. After washing it down with a swig of the sweet pear juice that came from a nearby orchard, he slammed his mug on the table and rushed from the room. His mother shook her head. *I really must work on his manners*, she thought.

Flying down the steps two at a time, Elkanah nearly tripped over the small sill on the bottom of the front door. He ran across the courtyard, sandals flopping, his tunic untied. It *couldn't* be true. Could Sha-Khohr be back? And completely healed? His father must be wrong.

He slid open the heavy wooden barn door and started inside. Elkanah was instantly overtaken by the dimness of the stable, the shard of sunlight streaming through a high window, and the smell of hay and manure and animal sweat. Running down the aisle between the stalls, he stopped at the last opening on the right. Standing there, munching hay and swinging his head to keep off the flies, was Sha-Khohr. Back safe. Unhurt.

Elkanah grabbed the colt's back leg and pulled up the hoof. What had been an oozing, nauseating crevice just yesterday morning was now dry and whole. The color was good. The little donkey didn't flinch when Elkanah pushed on the spot where the crack had been.

When had he reappeared? It must have been during the night or early morning. Elkanah stood silent for several minutes. Had he dreamed the whole thing? Maybe his ministrations to the little animal *had* been what made him better. But no ... he had worked with donkeys too long. He knew how slowly a disease like that healed.

Elkanah dropped to the straw along the wall of the stall and processed what he was sure of: His donkey had been crippled yesterday. Two strange men had come and taken him. He had followed them to check on Sha-Khohr and had run into another man, the one who had ridden the colt into Jerusalem. He knew all this to be true.

Looking up at the donkey's glossy, coal-black ears, Elkanah noticed something sticking to the wall. He got up, gently pushed Sha-Khohr's head aside, and moved in front of the beast. A parchment fragment was jammed behind one of the beams that descended from the ceiling and helped hold up the wall. Elkanah pulled it out and unrolled it.

"My master definitely had need of him. Now he is returned to you, safe and whole."

It was true, all of it! All this talk of that man being a Messiah—maybe there was something to it. Elkanah didn't know. All he knew was that Sha-Khohr was back and that he was never letting him go again.

He thought he might ride him over to Ruchel's home tomorrow evening. Perhaps she would sing for him.

———

It was a remarkably dry and dusty month. As Lilith stepped gingerly over a pile of donkey droppings in the middle of the thoroughfare, she thought about how the winter rains, usually so heavy and life-giving, had been brief and unproductive this spring. Surely there would be a drought.

All of which meant the spring fruits—the avocados and apricots, ordinarily so plump and juicy and displayed in cascading bursts of color—were smaller and pallid this year. Only the garlic, threaded into long braids and nailed to the vendors' booths, was as fresh and fragrant as always. Lilith made a note to buy several braids on her way home from the market.

Passover was always a time to look for the best—fruits, vegetables, honey, wines. Lilith took pride in her Passover feast, in seeing her entire family gathered around the table as the ritual began. Even Ezra and Shoshannah always seemed happy and content to be there. Their marriage, which had started out so rocky, had settled into a routine of mutual affection. So what if there wasn't a passionate love between the two? Lilith couldn't say passion had ever flared between her and Naahum, but they got along. They had built a business and a family, and that was enough ... wasn't it?

Lilith usually tried to block the memories of that horrible wedding: the lateness of the bride, the half-hearted efforts of the groom, the shortage of wine. At least that had been settled in the court—that moron, Jeremiah, had paid them for every jug of wine that hadn't been delivered. But even with that satisfaction, Lilith knew, deep in her heart, that the wedding would have been a debacle without the additional vintage that had shown up from ... well, who knew?

She didn't believe that ridiculous story about Mary's son waving his hands over some water jugs. Someone must have thought it would be a great joke to let the family think the wine was gone, then appear with some that had been held back. It didn't bear much thinking about. Lilith resolutely set it behind her.

The one pleasure that had come from that disastrous evening was seeing Mary again; they had kept their promises to see each other more often. Since the wedding, Mary had come to stay with Lilith, and Lilith had returned the visit and stayed in Nazareth. She remembered the odd interaction with Shoshannah before her trip. She'd pressed a very expensive and highly decorated tunic into Lilith's hands, for Mary to give to Yeshua.

Lilith had been a bit embarrassed. "Really, Shoshannah, you don't even know him. You don't need to do something so extravagant."

A rare spark of animation had lit Shoshannah's eyes. "I am so thankful to Yeshua for what he did at the wedding," she said. "It was incredibly kind."

Mary had been overjoyed at the gift of the tunic and laughed when she discovered Shoshannah had overheard her conversation with her wandering son. "He certainly can use it!" she had chuckled. "The next time he drops in, I'll make sure he gets it." Then her face grew wistful. "But he doesn't drop in very often."

The whole situation had been very strange. But then, Lilith reflected, *everything* concerning her daughter-in-law was so different than what she herself had experienced as a young bride. She chalked the gift of the tunic up to a burst of girlish enthusiasm.

And now Mary was in Jerusalem for the Passover! And oh, how Lilith had wanted to go along! Mary had pleaded with her and Naahum to make the week-long journey. For a moment, Lilith thought Naahum might agree. But in the end, he wouldn't leave his business, his home, the old men at the gate where he sat most days. And so they were, once again, stuck in Cana.

But how excited she was for Mary! Her younger sons had taken her for the feast, and she was sure Yeshua would be there as well. How nice the family could be together for the Passover! If anyone deserved to have her children around her, it was Mary.

Lilith needed to make her final purchases and get home. There was still so much to be done before the big day. She relished the idea of getting her silver candlesticks and crisp, white tablecloth out for the meal. In her head, she heard the blessings and songs of the ritual, and the readings that told the story of the people of Israel's redemption from Egypt. Tonight, the night before the Passover, Naahum would take a candle and lead the family to look in every nook and cranny of the house, in case any leaven remained. She remembered how excited Ezra would get as a child when he found a crumb or two that had been missed in the ritual cleaning. When the whole house had been gone over, Naahum would recite:

"All leaven that is in my possession, that which I have seen and that which I have not seen, be it null, be it accounted as the dust of the earth."

Then, and only then, would the house be clean for the feast.

Amid her reverie and plans and anxiety, Lilith didn't see the stone in the pathway between the fruit merchant and the old woman selling herbs. She stepped on it, and her right foot buckled, wrenching her ankle and bringing her down in a spasm of pain that ripped through her leg.

Lilith found herself rolling on the ground, her basket scattered, her tunic riding up, and her headdress slipping off. Despite the pain, she was most aware of her embarrassment, first of falling, then of making a display of herself in public. She yanked her tunic down to cover her legs and looked around to see who had noticed. Her basket had ended up several feet away, the apricots rolling about like game pieces.

Well, there is no dignified way to do this, she thought, as she brought herself to her knees, rising heavily onto her good leg and then gingerly testing her weight on the bad ankle. The leg buckled with a jolt of pain. It was obvious she should not walk on it, but what else could she do? Stand in the middle of the street, frozen like Lot's wife?

She was contemplating how to hobble a few feet to pick up her basket when a soft hand took her arm and a steady voice asked, "Are you all right? How can I help?"

Lilith turned to look at her savior and saw a small, dark-skinned girl with clear jet-black eyes gazing at her. Lilith knew her ... but how? She was disoriented and didn't know how to react. Lilith was a woman who helped others, not one who needed help herself.

"Oh, I am all right," she said with a sheepish laugh, dusting off her tunic as the girl held onto her arm. "If you could hand me my basket ... "

The girl stepped over to the basket, turned on its side, and began refilling it with the apricots. She handed it to Lilith. "I don't think your fruit is too badly bruised," she said.

"I'm sure it will be fine," Lilith blurted, wanting to get out of there but not trusting her ankle to hold her. "I'm sorry, but you look familiar ... have we met?"

The girl gave her a steady look, head high.

"I am Melea."

Melea? Lilith paused. Strange name. *Melea.* She knew that name, but how? As the girl continued to gaze at her, full recognition crashed onto Lilith.

Melea. The Samaritan girl. The girl who had turned Ezra's life upside down.

Melea could see the realization dawning on Lilith. Her amusement sparkled as she watched the conflicting emotions run across her almost-mother-in-law's face. Horror. Embarrassment. Guilt. A strong need to get away.

"Oh. It's you."

What a feeble thing to say, Lilith thought. *Couldn't I have thought of something better than that?*

She straightened to her full height and resumed her air of authority. "Thank you for the help," she said stiffly. Condescendingly. She made a move to hobble away, ankle or no ankle.

"I never held it against you, you know." Melea stood calmly, speaking in a soft, clear voice. "I loved your son, and I held out hope we could be together, but I knew deep down it could never work."

Lilith reared back in disgust. How dare this slip of a girl assume it might have worked at all? A Samaritan? How forward of her!

"Excuse me?" she barked. "How could you *ever* dare hope my son would marry outside his faith? Outside his people? To a ... a ... *Samaritan.*" She spat the word as if it burned her.

"How did I dare hope?" Melea repeated, smiling. "Love always hopes. And when you are young, everything seems possible." She stopped, quiet for a moment. "Ezra is a good man. I pray he is happy."

Lilith's face was a study in controlled fury. "He is *very* happy. His wife is a beautiful, accomplished woman. He certainly does not need your best wishes. And I don't need your forgiveness."

She lurched around, ignoring the shooting pain in her ankle. Only pride would get her to the end of the street, away from this girl, who seemed so self-controlled in the face of Lilith's anger. Her hate, really. Lilith knew deep in herself she was being unfair, but her beliefs were deeply ingrained. And so it would be.

Lilith turned her head when she heard the running steps and voice of a child behind her. "Mother, look what the fruit man gave me!" A young boy held out a peach that was slightly wilted. "He said I could have it!"

"Well, aren't you the lucky one?" Melea said, bending over to run her hand through his ginger curls. "I hope you said thank you." She looked up at Lilith, holding her eyes, not saying anything.

Recognition hit Lilith like a bolt of lightning. This child standing before her appeared to be about two years old. And he was Ezra, down to the stocky little body, the high voice, the babyish curls. *Dear Adonai, he had a child with her. Does he know? Does Shoshannah know? Does Naahum know? Am I the only one who didn't?*

Not a word passed between the women. Victory shone in Melea's eyes, a confidence that all the bile-soaked words flung at her by the older woman were now null and void. The young mother reached down, took her son's hand—now sticky with peach juice—and turned. They walked slowly back to the fruit seller's stand.

Lilith limped to a tree stump thirty paces down the dusty street and collapsed. What a fool she had been. A secret life under her nose. She had no control over anything and had probably been laughed at all this time. What did that make her?

———

It had been months since Deborah was dragged from her home to go before the Pharisees. She was living on the other side of that nightmare, moving toward a place of hope.

All her grief over Aaron's death, her tumultuous relationship with Seneca, her disgrace before her family, her mother's pleading and screaming and begging, her degradation when facing her own death by stoning … and then to be rescued. It had truly been a rebirth.

After the Master—that's how she thought of him now—had picked her up, literally, from the dust of the street, she'd felt a lightness she had never known before. And it wasn't just that she had been spared a horrible death. The guilt that had lain on her soul was lifted, just as the Master had raised her in his arms.

Soon the question became, *Where will Deborah go?* She could not bear going back to her family, people she loved who had stood in the doorway watching her being dragged out. Who had gone to the Pharisees? Would she spend the rest of her life suspecting her father? Her brother? She could not enter that house and live under their authority again.

The Master had listened to her broken sobs and offered a solution. He would take her to his friends, Mary and Martha, and their brother, Lazarus, who lived in Bethany, just over an hour's walk outside the city. She accepted the offer gratefully, but as they got closer to the house, Deborah panicked. Would they accept her? Even with the Master to vouch for her, would they declare her an outcast?

It appeared the Master's friends were used to odd requests and strange people showing up at their door. Mary, the younger sister, showed Deborah to a spare room and even offered to share some clothing with her until her own could be cleaned. The room was spartan, quiet, with little more than a mat and a table for a candle. But Deborah fell onto the bed gratefully and slept through the night.

The next morning, it was obvious the siblings were curious about her. The Master had left, so Deborah could not give him a final thank-you. Martha was circumspect about her questions, but Mary could not contain her interest.

"So how do you know him?" she asked urgently, as if this were the most important thing she needed to know. Deborah looked at her blankly. "The Master—how do you know him?"

How did one explain their gratitude to someone who had literally saved their life?

"It's a long story," Deborah began slowly. She took a drink of watered wine. "Really, it's hard to talk about."

Martha, who seemed to be a no-nonsense person, interrupted. "You don't need to explain anything," she said brusquely. "Mary, don't bother her. She'll tell us when she's ready." Deborah looked at her gratefully.

In the days that followed, Deborah fell into the household routine and gleaned more about the Master's strange doings and miraculous feats. It appeared he had a group of men—disciples—who traveled with him around the country as he preached and taught. If the stories were to be believed, the Master also healed the sick and made food enough for ten people stretch to five thousand. The sisters saw themselves as his "home base," a place where he could come to rest—to get away from the crowds, be fed, and catch up on sleep. A place where he was nurtured and made strong enough to go back out on the road.

Deborah became part of this rhythm, and as she cleaned and cooked and helped make beds, she learned about all this amazing man had done. Healed lepers. Preached what was considered heresy in the synagogues. Calmed an entire storm when he and his disciples were in a boat at sea. Mary whispered about something involving her brother, Lazarus—Deborah was never quite sure what had happened—that he had been dead and then raised? That seemed preposterous, and every time Mary wanted to talk about it, Martha would find her out and end the conversation with a sharp, "Mary. There are some things that are not ours to discuss." Every time Deborah looked at the dreamy young man, Lazarus—who seemed to be lost in his own world—she wondered about the truth of the matter.

The Master never talked about these things, but when his followers showed up at the house—with or without him—they would regale everyone with the latest wonders. And at the heart of all of it was this truth: This man was going to beat back the oppression of the Romans. Everything he had done so far was wonderful, but the best was yet to come, according to one of the followers, a man named Peter. Yeshua was going to usher in the Kingdom of God!

Hearing about the Romans made Deborah's heart shrink and her stomach roil. How could she forget Seneca? Every day her tunic grew a bit tighter, and the evidence of his part in her life became clearer. Slowly, she had shared bits of her experience with the sisters. Once her condition became obvious, she told them about Seneca and the battle that had raged with her family to palm off the child on another man. Then she finally told them of the nightmarish scene that had taken place in a dusty, dead-end alley in Jerusalem.

Deborah was happy enough to fit into this little family, and they seemed content to let her stay, as she was a hard worker and a quiet soul. *Mary chatters enough for us all,* Deborah thought with a smile. She was a cheerful sort who didn't let much get her down. Martha did the worrying for all of them, always fretting about money and food and keeping the house clean.

Martha told Deborah she was a bit annoyed Yeshua and his followers would not be celebrating the Passover with them. How she loved receiving them with herb-scented water to wash their feet and serving them her best food on beautiful dishes. It was a letdown to have only the four of them around the Passover table this year, but Martha knew

Yeshua had his reasons. Perhaps he and his disciples would stop over in the days following the feast.

The week dragged on half-heartedly, the family going through the motions even at the height of the popular feast. Still, it was exciting to see the many pilgrims and worshippers pass their home on their way to Jerusalem. They came from everywhere—a babel of tongues, skins of every color, exotic clothing—all heading to the Temple to worship and sacrifice. Occasionally a traveler would stop at the house and ask for a drink of water. On those days, Deborah couldn't help being pulled into the festive atmosphere.

It was late the night before the Passover—after the women had completed all the household chores and Lazarus had finished feeding and bedding the animals—when a crashing sound came at the door. The urgent banging froze everyone in their places. No one knocked like that late at night unless there was trouble.

Lazarus got to the door first and pulled it open cautiously, peering around the corner to see who was there. Mark, one of Yeshua's younger disciples, pushed through the door, ignoring the startled faces of those inside.

"He's been arrested!" he gasped, his hands on his knees as he struggled to breathe. His sweat-stained clothing made it clear he had been running.

"Who?" Mary asked, running forward, though everyone knew the answer.

"The Master!" Mark cried. "We had dinner together tonight and then went out to the Mount of Olives. The authorities came out and arrested him. We think they've hauled him over to Caiaphas."

"On what charges?" Martha's voice was level. "What did they arrest him for?"

Mark waved his hand. "Oh, who knows? They've been out to get him for a long time. Something about heresy and betraying the Roman government and being a traitor, but really, they just want him out of the way. It's something the Sanhedrin cooked up, we're sure, but ... "

"What do we do now?" Martha asked calmly. "Or maybe, what *can* we do now? Can we bring him anything? Where are the other disciples?"

"I don't know. I just don't know." No one was sure if Mark was replying to the first part of Martha's question or the second. "We should know by morning if Caiaphas is keeping him. They may just want to scare him ... scare *us*."

"Where are the disciples now?" Martha asked again. Coldly.

Mark looked up, sheepish and dismayed. "I don't know. Everyone took off—we all scattered. The soldiers came, with swords and torches, and that damned Judas—we all knew he was cooking up something—he gave Yeshua up to them! If we can get our hands on him ... "

Mark trailed off, distraught and exhausted.

Lazarus leaned down to meet Mark's eyes. "Are you afraid they'll arrest you disciples, too?"

"No, not really ... " Mark stopped and stood up straight. "Yes, I suppose we are. You know how that goes sometimes. Stop the leader and take the followers. Some of us have families. Peter … he's got a wife and kids and a mother-in-law to support." He paused. "And you, you're not necessarily safe either. Everyone knows the Master is your friend, and that we stay here. They could come after you, too."

Deborah had been standing stock-still, feeling like she was watching herself from outside her body. The words "Roman government" had sent her reeling. She and everyone in that room knew what the Romans did to traitors. A niggling thought in the back of her mind made her wonder if Seneca could do anything to stop it.

Would he, even if he could?

Martha had once again taken charge. After telling Mark he should stay for the night, she marched briskly around the kitchen, packing things into a large bag.

"We'll leave in the morning and find out what we can," she said. "We'll bring some things for Yeshua if he's in jail. We will be there for him." She looked pointedly again at Mark, then softened. "Thank you for coming to tell us," she said gently. "Now, go to bed."

The day was barely breaking when Martha, Mary, and Deborah set out for Jerusalem. Mark had left hours earlier, telling them about the upper room they had used the previous evening for their feast and giving the address.

"Perhaps some of the disciples and other women will be there," he said.

The following hours were a wearying, maddening fight to find out anything about what was happening to Yeshua. Evidently, he had been released from Caiaphas' court early that morning and sent over to Pontius Pilate. Hearing that name had made everyone's stomachs rise into their throats. If this had gone beyond the Jewish Sanhedrin, it was serious. Getting the Romans involved was always a bad sign.

Standing outside Pilate's palace, the crowds swirled in celebration of the upcoming festival. The three women were once again foiled when a guard on the front steps told them Yeshua had been moved to Herod's court. And then they were stunned when the guard told them a death sentence had been passed. How could this happen—and so quickly? How had they missed it? They had pledged to be there for Yeshua, and instead they were standing uselessly in a doorway with a bag of supplies while he faced execution.

After conversing among themselves, they decided to head to the upper room to see who else was there and what they knew. The courtyard appeared deserted, but as the trio climbed the indoor stairs, they could hear soft voices in the room above. There sat the women they had heard about and met once or twice, who also ministered to Yeshua and the disciples: Mary, Salome, and Mary, Yeshua's mother. Martha, Mary, and Deborah sat down beside them, hugging and clutching one another's hands. They might not have known each other well, but they all loved Yeshua and wanted to give back to him for what he had brought into their lives. For one, he had healed a sick child. For another, he had brought her brother back from the dead. For another ... he was her son.

And Yeshua had given Deborah her life again—literal life as well as spiritual life, a family life, a reason to live. They were all in this together. The women who loved him.

Deborah couldn't help noticing it was only the women who were there.

———

Maret's family had been camped outside Jerusalem for three days. Tired, footsore, and weary to the soul, they had finally traipsed into the city, heading for the pastures to the west, where thousands of other pilgrims were also setting up camp. Maret had to admit these three days had been a balm to her soul—being able to wash clothing and bodies; having true meals that weren't eaten in haste; watching her son grow stronger after his bout of bowel sickness. She had even found herself laughing with the women in the tents as they watched their children band into a play group almost immediately. *Children are children everywhere,* she thought. Even with different languages and customs and skin colors, they bonded, running around the camp and getting into mischief even with a thousand eyes on them.

That morning, Simon had asked her if she'd do the trip again. Maret wasn't sure at first. The excitement of friends and neighbors waving them off, of planning and packing and poring over maps … all of that had faded with the reality of the road and the dangers they had encountered. This was her one trip, she finally concluded, one she would never attempt again. So she would make the most of it.

Maret had been dreading the return to Cyrene, even though they wouldn't have to be on a schedule. The unending desert, the dust, the strange wanderers on the road ... she didn't want to face any of it, though she tried to keep her anxiety to herself. Simon had enough to take care of without her added fears.

That's why she'd been so surprised and delighted when Simon announced that morning that they would not be taking the desert road back to Cyrene. Instead, they would be taking a ship. After the Passover, they would travel for a few days to the port of Jaffa and board a ship to Cyrene, one that would bring them to the city in about a week. There were still dangers at sea, of course—the spring weather could bring storms. But they would be traveling close enough to the shoreline to seek cover from the anger of a tempest.

A water trip was expensive, but her husband must have known Maret could not face a sick child, strange campmates, and treacherous river crossings again, especially since they would be loaded down with so many "treasures" for their friends and family.

They had spent yesterday in the great city collecting the items their neighbors had asked for. Spices and potions, salts and herbs ... Maret had found it all except a gift for old Miriam. She had said Maret would know it when she saw it—something from the land. Maret was stumped and had certainly seen nothing she thought would interest the older woman. She might have to return to the vendor's stall outside the Fish

Gate and purchase that beautiful rock she had seen yesterday, one with the colors of the desert sunset.

She quickly finished cleaning the breakfast dishes and stored the lentil pottage for another meal. Simon had promised to take her and the boys to the Temple this morning in preparation for the Passover. The line for slaughtering animals would probably be too long for them to make an official sacrifice, but they wanted to pray in the Temple courts along with thousands of others on this special day. The Passover would officially begin that evening, and already Maret had joined several other families in purchasing a portion of lamb for their evening meal.

Maret caught a blur of little-boy flesh in the corner of her eye. Rufus and Alexander were running wild with a herd of other little boys, like a pack of jackals in the desert. She didn't really blame them—they had been so patient and obedient on the long journey, and just to see Alexander healthy did her heart good. Nevertheless, they needed to come and get ready for the day at the Temple.

Maret waylaid her sons as they tripped across the tent pegs in a game of chase with four other children. "Stop!" she commanded. "You need to come in and get ready. Father is taking us to the Temple, remember?"

Rufus looked woefully at his friends speeding off before him. "Can we stop at the shop with the animals?" he beseeched his mother, turning pleading brown eyes on her.

Maret laughed. They had stopped by that particular shop yesterday, and the boys were fascinated by the many exotic animals sold there—peacocks to grace a king's courtyard; a monkey from the Arabias that sat on the vendor's shoulder; snakes that curled in their baskets, waiting for a passing caravan to buy them and take them farther east.

"We'll see how much time we have. But the purpose of this trip is to be at the Temple during the Passover. There will be many, *many* people there, and you must stay with us, so you don't get lost."

The boys disappeared into their tent and quickly washed up and changed their clothes. Simon appeared from behind the other tents, where he had been exchanging the latest news with the other men. It was truly a Tower of Babel in this camp; many languages were represented, but there was usually someone who could translate. And to think—all these people worshipped the same Yahweh! All were people of the promise!

Maret, Simon, and the boys set off, with promises from the family next door to watch their tent and possessions. They had a day with nothing to buy, nothing required of them other than praying and worshipping and taking in the grandeur of Solomon's Temple. This was what they had come to do. This was what the trip was all about.

They entered the Sheep's Gate with hundreds of other pilgrims. Though the highlight of the week was, of course, celebrating the Passover in the Holy City and visiting the Temple, Maret couldn't suppress her excitement at being among so many people from so many countries. Though they had done most of their shopping yesterday, she couldn't help stopping at a booth offering salts—for cooking, for bathing, for curing ailments—the variety seemed endless. She made note of the location so they could stop on the way back. She didn't want to haul a parcel of salt around all day.

The boys, as usual, were in a frenzy of excitement. Keeping track of them was a constant struggle as they darted this way and that, around a vendor hawking freshly baked flat-bread; past a young woman assisting an elderly man, nearly plowing into them in the process.

"Rufus! Alexander!" Maret called to them across the narrow lane. "Stay with us. Now!"

The boys made their way back to their parents, abashed for a few moments before spying something else that made them take off.

They had made little headway toward the Temple; the streets were just too congested. Suddenly, the crowd before Maret seemed to part in much the same way she imagined the Red Sea had for Moses. What was going on? Was there a large vehicle coming through, perhaps a team of donkeys hauling a wagon?

At her first glimpse of the bright red cape and flashing helmet, Maret recoiled. Roman soldiers. Whatever were *they* doing in this teeming area of the city, one largely peopled by vendors and their customers? As she grabbed Alexander by the shoulder and pulled him into the overhang of a fruit stall, she saw Simon doing the same across the lane with Rufus. The more out of sight they were, the better.

The soldier marched past them, spear upright and at the ready, staring straight ahead. Evidently something was following him, as the crowd remained pressed against the buildings and shops. Surely something really impressive was happening. Maret peered across the lane and saw Rufus' wide eyes, Simon with a firm grip on his arm.

Nothing happened for a few moments. Then Maret heard something being dragged on the rough cobblestones of the lane, followed by a harsh voice. She held her breath and clasped Alexander's shoulder so tightly he whimpered in pain. Around the corner about a block away, she saw a piece of wood protruding from a side street, followed by a person bowed under its weight, covered with blood. *Surely this isn't happening, today of all days?* Maret had heard of the ghastly crucifixions the Romans used to punish rebels, but she had never seen one. Though Cyrene was also under Roman authority, the oversight there was mostly benign, almost nonchalant, and the ruler and the ruled coexisted more or less peacefully.

All the horrors of their journey paled in comparison to this gruesome sight. Maret found herself unable to move, pasted to the spot as if the sticky substance she used to repair a broken pot were gluing her sandals to the ground. Who was this wretch who shuffled along, carrying a heavy crossbar that would be his method of execution? What had he done to deserve this treatment?

Two other soldiers followed him, whips in hand, seeming to delight in the cruelty of flicking the man when they deemed he was moving too slowly. Not that you could tell if they were doing any damage—he was already a mass of blood, hardly human. On his head, he wore a few clumps of what looked like thorns; his hands were slick with sweat, clutching the large chunk of wood. As he drew closer, Maret could hear his heavy breathing, ragged and uneven. He looked down at his feet, as if making sure they were still moving.

"He doesn't look so good now, does he?" one of the soldiers bellowed to the crowd, pointing the whip at the man's back. "Not much of a conqueror, is he?"

No one made a sound. The man's broken body, barely covered with a loincloth, shambled forward inches at a time. The wooden beam dragged behind him, the sound rasping harshly through the narrow lane. Maret stared in horror, then saw Simon turning Rufus around, his back to the lane, and covering his ears.

In a few minutes, the poor creature was close enough Maret could have stretched out her hand to touch him. She silently prayed that he would move along, pass them, become someone else's horror. And then the rasping drag stopped. The man swayed a bit but did not move. The soldier on his right prodded him with his whip, just as Maret had seen livestock pushed along at market. Even that much seemed to upset the man's fragile balance. As if in slow motion, he fell over, the beam falling across his side and chest, then landing with a resounding thump on the cobblestones.

The crowd gasped as one. What happened now? Would they whip the man while he was down? Would it help?

The two soldiers conferred with each other. Maret saw both were middle-aged, with the craggy, leather-like faces of men who had been in the sun for long periods of time. Eventually they seemed to come to a decision. Their eyes peered around the crowd, looking for something ... or someone. Everyone dropped their gaze from the soldiers, not wanting to be singled out for whatever they were planning.

"You!" The same soldier who had been taunting the crowd earlier yelled. "You!"

Maret lifted her eyes uneasily, wondering whom the soldier was addressing. A wave of cold sweat hit her when she saw him pointing the whip directly at Simon. Her husband was confused, looking around to as if to make sure the soldier was really speaking to him.

"I said *you!*" the soldier barked, pulling Simon by the arm into the street, leaving Rufus standing alone, bewildered and crying. "We don't have all day, so you're going to help carry this beam."

Simon looked as if he'd been paralyzed, but then the soldier roughly pushed him toward the splintered piece of wood. "Pick it up!" he commanded. "Let's go!"

With a pleading glance toward Maret, Simon reached down and hoisted the beam up off the street, settling it on his shoulder. Maret could already see the blood from the beam soaking into the cloth of Simon's tunic. Her hand went to her mouth as she tried to keep herself from vomiting. All around people were dumbstruck, some crying, and most notably, some acting as if this were something they witnessed every day. And maybe it was. Maybe this city she had been so excited to see was nothing but a death trap.

Simon took a tentative step forward, trying not to hit the man on the ground with the beam. The soldier who hadn't yet spoken yanked the man to his feet and pushed him toward Simon, who reached out a hand to steady him.

"Don't touch him!" the first soldier said. "He's a dog on his way to his death!"

Simon took small, steady steps down the lane toward the city gate. The condemned man shambled behind him, already half dead, head down, breathing heavily. When they were several paces away, the crowd started milling in the lane again, filling the space. Rufus ran to his mother and raised his tear-stained, imploring face to her.

"Should we follow them?" he asked. "Should we run behind them?"

Alexander answered since Maret could not speak. "No, Father wouldn't want us to do that. There's nothing we can do. He'll be back, and we'll wait for him here."

He steered his mother toward a bench next to the fruit seller's stall. He took a few coins from his pocket, bought a cup of fruit juice from the vendor, and offered it to Maret. She sat quietly, mutely, staring at the street and the bustling crowds, the people stepping right on the patch of bloody stones as if it were any other market day. Stepping on top of the piece of wood that had chipped off the beam when it hit the ground.

In a trance, Maret rose from her seat and pushed through the crowd to the middle of the lane. Reaching down, she carefully placed her hand on the blood-stained stones and closed her eyes, as if drawing something from them. Then she picked up the little chunk of wood, with its ragged, splintered edge and crimson stain.

Miriam had said she'd know it when she saw it. She was right.

—

Seneca couldn't wait for all these blasted foreigners to go back home. Jerusalem was awash with them. Parthians, Medes, Elamites, Cappadocians, Arabs, Libyans … all those barbarian languages and smells and odd clothing. Ruling over the Judeans the rest of the year was bad enough, with their bloody Temple rituals and pious priests.

But at least we understand each other, he thought. *We rule them, and they obey. For the most part.*

Jerusalem had hit its limit with the ceaseless crowds this afternoon, the last day of the week. Once three stars had appeared in the sky, the Jewish Sabbath would begin. Then, suddenly, the packed streets would be deserted as the throngs locked themselves in—where, exactly, he didn't know and didn't particularly care. He had heard of families renting out extra rooms above their lodgings for the pilgrims to use. Then tomorrow, their day of rest, and by the next day, they would be hauling themselves out of the city and toward their homes. What a relief that would be.

But first, a distasteful task. Three crucifixions outside of town … three Jewish dogs hanging from a tree on their Sabbath eve, no less. Seneca couldn't help but wonder at the chief priest's urgency in having them crucified so quickly. Why not wait until next week? An execution today meant the bodies would have to be taken down before the Sabbath began, and the condemned might not even be dead yet. Then the soldiers would have to break the poor devils' legs so their bodies dropped and they suffocated. Sounded awful, but Seneca had seen men on crosses so ready to die that suffocation was a mercy, really.

He usually didn't have to attend to this loathsome display. But a top soldier needed to trudge outside the city to give permission to the standing guards to finish the job if the prisoners took too long to die. Today, that lot had fallen to him.

He set off from his barracks, noticing that the sky was dusky, obscuring a weak sun. Seneca had lived through dust storms in this godforsaken hole, but this was different. There was no dust plugging his nose and throat, only an eerie, shadowy light. Even the birds had quit chirping, as if they sensed night approaching.

Seneca skirted the area outside the city where Deborah lived. At least, he thought she was still living there. In the weeks since it had happened, he'd tried to forget how he had hidden in shame in the alley and watched her disgrace and salvation. The heap of rags on the ground. The strange man writing in the dust. Their absorbed conversation as they walked past Seneca's hiding spot. Better to forget it. After all, Seneca was the conqueror, she the conquered. She'd known what she was getting into. If he had shirked some of his responsibility, he could live with it.

There was nothing I could have done to make the situation better, he heatedly reminded himself. At least, that's what he thought in the dark of the night. In the glare of daylight, he almost managed to convince himself that perhaps Deborah had deserved what was coming. It was, after all, her god that accused her—not his.

Seneca was approaching the stinking garbage heaps of Golgotha—also called "The Skull"—an outcropping of cliff that some thought looked like a death head. Personally, Seneca thought the stench and constant fires, as this was where they burned the refuse of the city, probably accounted for the name as much as anything else.

What a miserable place to die, he thought, then amended, *I guess there's no good place to die—why not here?*

Three crosses had been hoisted that morning, and the crucifixions were a good five hours in. The odd darkness seemed to thicken. It was velvety, almost like a fog. The sun tried to peer through the murkiness, but only appeared as a sickly pale ball. Seneca could barely see the crosses as he started up the hill. The way the dark blotch on the left-hand cross was hanging told him that criminal was already gone. But the men on the middle cross and the one to the right still moved feebly.

Time to finish this show, whoever these poor bastards are—or were.

It always sickened Seneca to see how many people stood around the spectacle of death, enjoying it. Of course, the righteous Temple-mongers were there, looking smug, nodding together at a job well done. One of these men was probably some heretic the priests had goaded Pontius Pilate into killing. Those black birds of doom had no power on their own to have a person executed, but they could make a stir about someone they wanted out of the way—resurrecting stories of treason against the empire, tidbits they'd overheard the miscreant say about rejecting taxation. Whether the accusations were true or not, it wasn't too difficult to throw a bone the priests' way now and then. Keeping them happy was a small price to pay.

Also present, of course, were the victims' friends and family, usually standing at a distance, not willing to be associated with the crimes of the dying. More often than not, there was no one at all, and the man hanging on the tree died alone in the world. But today, there was a cluster of women some way off. *How horrible for them. Why don't they just stay home until it's over?*

Seneca was breathing hard as he crested the hill. *Too much time sitting around doing paperwork is making me soft,* he thought. He saw the soldiers on duty doing what they usually did on a long watch—drinking and gambling. Though drinking was strictly forbidden while a soldier was on duty, an exception was made for this terrible job. Seneca remembered the first couple of times he had been assigned to a crucifixion—how he had vomited at the smells, the flies, the pitiful groans. He wouldn't begrudge any soldier some wine. He had quickly learned to block out the world, to stop his ears to the groans and pleading, to drink and drink hard.

"Never look them in the eye," a war-hardened veteran had told him. "They're not people. They're hunks of meat hanging in a butcher shop."

Seneca approached the men crouched on the flat, rocky spot on the top of the hill. They had abandoned the wine and were absorbed in their second-favorite activity, gambling. Oftentimes, there wasn't anything worth gambling over in the accuseds' possessions. These scruffy, hard-luck types went out of the world as they came in—naked and with nothing. But once in a while, there would be a piece of clothing worth vying for, or a trinket being carried by the doomed.

Today had brought better luck. One of the soldiers—Seneca never could remember their names—had a pair of dice and was tossing it in a bid to claim a handsome-looking tunic. Unusual that someone dying this kind of death would have something so valuable. It was a buff brown, a high-quality wool, and all of a piece with no seams. That was rare, even for Romans, as the cost of a piece of fabric that size was out of the grasp of most citizens.

As Seneca considered the tunic, the soldier who had been tossing the dice whooped in excitement and grasped it to himself. Standing up, a little unsteadily, he threw it around his shoulders and strode back, showing off in front of his two chagrined comrades who had lost. His hoots and gibes grew increasingly raucous, fueled by the strong purple wine.

Seneca noticed that the back of the tunic dipped lower than the front and, strangely enough, was embroidered with flowers.

He peered closer at the soldier wearing it, who pirouetted in front of him like an Arabian dancer. They were … lilies.

How strange, he thought. *Why would someone with the means to purchase such a fine piece of material and do such beautiful needlework give a tunic to someone who was a traitor to the state? Surely this man couldn't have afforded it on his own?*

For the first time, Seneca raised his eyes to the skeletal figure hanging on the middle cross. Evidently the authorities had had some fun with this one. He was wearing a crown made of the locust thorns that grew outside the city. Nasty, sharp, long menaces that could tear your skin if you weren't careful. Nailed to the top of the vertical board of the cross was a piece of parchment. The darkness, coupled with the breeze that ruffled the parchment's corners, obscured the words. Seneca leaned over to the soldier who was still proudly wearing the hard-won tunic and asked what the sign said.

"It's something Pilate told us to put up there." The soldier shrugged. "Says, 'The King of the Jews.' The priests didn't like *that* at all," he confided, nodding to the tightly clumped group. "But Pilate said we had to leave it."

What a humiliating thing to have nailed above your implement of death, Seneca thought. Poor, deluded bastard must have really riled up the authorities, if he thought he was a king. But most of the time, these criminals deserved their fates. What did they think was going to happen when they went up against the most powerful empire in the world?

Dropping his eyes from the sign, Seneca let them fall on the creature hanging there. Half-dead. *More* than half-dead.

Barely moving as the flies burrowed into the wounds on his hands and feet, twitching as muscle spasms ran across his body. This man, if you could still call him that, was about to die. They might not have to break his legs after all.

As Seneca gazed at the man's bowed head, studded by thorns and covered in matted hair and patches of blood, he suddenly raised his face, eyes closed, and muttered to himself. *Probably delirious*, Seneca thought, the fever that wracked crucifixion victims taking over his brain in the final moments. But as the whispering went on, it began to sound like a chant. Maybe the man was praying? Fat lot of good that would do him.

Suddenly the man's eyes opened and bore straight into Seneca's face. Those eyes. He knew them. Where? He took a step back, unable to break the man's gaze. Out of nowhere, Seneca felt his gut gripped by a realization: This was the man who had rescued Deborah from the angry mob. He never would have recognized him in his pathetic state, but those eyes … they were the eyes of the man who had shown compassion by standing up to that arrogant, god-stuffed crowd, with their clenched fists and upraised stones.

In that instant, Seneca knew the wretch on the cross recognized him, too. There was a look of pity on his face, even as he grunted and moaned and twitched, hanging there—in the words of that old soldier—like a slab of meat in the butcher's shop. This man actually felt sorry for him! Seneca staggered backward, tripping over a boulder and almost crashing into the circle of soldiers who were now glazed with boredom and tired of their drinking and gambling. He had to get away, away from this man who had seen through him and who had seen through Deborah. Away from this whole nasty business of death and stink and rottenness.

But he stood rooted, unable to move. The man hanging from the cross dropped his head again, letting a whoosh of breath escape from his sunken lungs. With great effort, he deliberately lifted his head again, summoning up the little air he could pull into his slowly suffocating body. The darkness had intensified, swirling almost palpably around the three crosses. Seneca remembered paintings from his childhood that depicted the Land of the Dead, the god of the underworld. Pluto, guarding his realm jealously. The darkness. The worms that writhed on the ground. The three-headed dog, Cerberus, that had the body of a snake. The images had terrified him, but this nightmarish scene rivaled those paintings in every way. The stink of despair. The far-off flames of the garbage fires, backlighting the crosses almost demonically. With a desperate final breath—almost a howl—the man gasped ...

"It. Is. Finished!"

Then his head lolled onto his chest and he was still.

Seneca gulped, watching the man's very spirit leave his body. He had been present at many such deaths, but none had affected him like this. Surely this man could not have been a criminal? His kindness was palpable, even in this wretched situation. Seneca felt cleansed, as if everything he had been done over the past months had suddenly come into sharp relief. Out of the swirling, hellish background of his surroundings and the thoughts in his head, one thing became clear.

He did not know how he would do it, but he would support Deborah and her child. He would not abandon her. He would find her—today. He would, someday, tell her about her attempted stoning that he had not been meant to see, how he had once again come across this strange man in his dying hours. That was what he must do, despite the consequences. He would face his responsibilities like a man.

He thought again of the look the creature on the cross had given him, one that hollowed him out and made all things known.

"Surely, he was a righteous man," Seneca murmured. He could not have been otherwise.

—

The day lay heavy over the city. A strange day … dark at noontime, as if a desert dust storm had rolled in, without the grit and mess.

If I were a superstitious man, Isaac thought, *I would say it was supernatural.* But instead, he reckoned it to be one of those odd coverings of the sun that happened sometimes. The wise men said these events were normal in the course of the heavens.

Isaac rushed through his chores. It was the last day of the week, but not a regular Sabbath. When the *shofar* sounded in just a few hours, it would be the Passover. He laughed as he thought of how he'd left Leah at home that morning—in a frenzy of cleaning, removing every particle of yeast in the house. Then she would prepare food for the feast as well as shake out and smooth the festive clothing the family would wear when they gathered that evening. It was probably just as well if he didn't head home too quickly.

And there was so much to do at the Temple. The oil in all the lamps needed to be replenished. Visitors had been constant for the past week, culminating in a massive crowd that very day—throngs from all over the world! Even with the crowds and the added work, Isaac enjoyed this week of the year, when Jews gathered in Jerusalem, some of them having traveled hundreds of miles. They often couldn't understand each other, but the language of sacrifice and tribute was the same everywhere.

Only one thing had marred this week—that strange meeting with Yeshua that had kept him up at night and put him in a strained position with the priests at the Temple. He had been seen leaving the courtyard with the young man, and they wanted to know why. Where had they gone? What had he said?

Isaac was vague. He did not mention this man was the boy who had been at the Temple twenty years ago—a boy some of them remembered. He simply said the man who had made such a mess in the courtyard was a troubled soul who had needed a place to sit and cool off. After that, they left him alone. He hoped they would let the matter drop.

But Isaac himself could not dismiss it: how Yeshua had muttered that this was a very hard week for him; how he'd despaired the misuse of the Court of the Gentiles; how he had been struck by the old Temple curtain. What had happened to him? In an ordinary week, Isaac could have kept tabs on a man who had made such a spectacle of himself. But when more than 150,000 people were milling around—and with him stuck in the Temple keeping up with the needs of the crowds—he had been unable to do little more than slip home for a few hours' sleep before returning.

It was the final hours before he would close the Temple for the festival. Last-minute visitors were wandering about, in and out of the courtyard, taking in the beauty of the interior, the rich tapestry of the curtain closing off the Holy of Holies, storing the sights in their minds so they could share them with friends and neighbors who couldn't make the journey. Isaac headed toward the alms container near the door, where pilgrims placed their donations. He needed to get it emptied and under lock and key before closing up.

Isaac took two steps and felt the floor shift under him. Was he sick? Perhaps he was dizzy from overwork and little sleep. But no, while the floor continued to tilt, Isaac heard a rumble—low and deep and far away. He stumbled to the nearest bench, not even thinking to look around and see how others were faring.

Isaac had experienced an earthquake once when he was a lad. He had been outdoors at his father's vineyard, walking through the rows of grapes, when suddenly a trembling started under his feet. Terrified, he had run back toward the house, thinking perhaps the earth itself would open up and swallow him. When he arrived home, the farm animals were running in circles, bellowing and squawking in terror. His mother had thrown her apron over her face in fear. As Isaac hugged his mother, he noticed the tremors had stopped. Later, he and his mother had had a good laugh as they took stock of any damage, finding none—if they didn't count the clay bowl that had fallen from the top shelf, its shards decorating the floor.

But whatever was happening now didn't seem like that earthquake. Isaac didn't remember any sound, just motion. Now, the distant rumble became louder, growing closer. The floor of the Temple blurred, the pattern of the tiles shaking. A woman screamed in the courtyard. A large urn standing next to the door, one used for ceremonial washing, tilted to the right and fell over in slow motion. Isaac felt like he was watching the scene from outside himself, as the urn cracked into a dozen pieces and water sloshed everywhere.

Dear Yahweh, what is happening? he silently prayed, clutching the arm of the bench tightly. He should be up and ministering to these people, not paralyzed with fright. But try as he might, he couldn't make one muscle move. The sound of thunder rolled in like a camel train, like the crash of waves in a storm. When it was at its loudest—and Isaac was sure the entire Temple would fall to pieces, much like Samson pulling down the pillars in Philistia—at that moment, another sound began. At first, Isaac couldn't tell where it was coming from. It sounded like a heavy piece of fabric was tearing with great difficulty.

Isaac jerked his eyes up to the curtain protecting the Holy of Holies, a double-layered piece of fabric that separated the people and even the priests from the unbearable and awesome holiness of Yahweh. Only once a year, on the Day of Atonement, did the high priest enter this sacred space and atone for the people with the blood of a ram or calf. Absolutely no one else could enter—why, even the high priest had a rope tied around his torso in case he died while communing with Yahweh and had to be pulled back out. No one else entered the Holy of Holies. Ever.

Isaac watched the two layers of the curtain as they trembled. The fabric was richly decorated with angels and winged creatures and disembodied eyes—the eyes of the Holy One. It had cost many *denarii*, he was sure, and what he saw and heard now convinced Isaac he was hallucinating. That curtain—that thick, solid length of tapestry—was ripping down the middle of each panel, slowly tearing between the embroidered two-winged creatures. The gash inched all the way to the bottom, as if an invisible pair of scissors traversed its length. The torn fabric hung limply, revealing the interior. In a daze, Isaac stood and walked toward the Holy of Holies, his eyes adjusting to the dimness of the little room he had never seen before.

It was empty, nothing there. Although he knew it would be empty, witnessing it shocked him. He remembered Yeshua's words earlier that week.

"To see the people of God being held back from Him by a curtain— how has Israel come to this?"

Isaac coughed and waved away fibers from the curtain, floating in the air like so many dust motes. He bent over, hands on his knees, and pondered what had just happened.

It seems the train of His robe has finally filled the Temple.

Running over Yeshua's words, Isaac moaned, tears streaming down his face.

"No more," he whispered. "Yeshua was right. No more will Yahweh be contained behind a curtain."

———

The day flew by in a flurry of preparations. Ruchel soon forgot about the odd man and his dramatics in the courtyard. Once, while crossing the wide space to bring a load of sheets to the housemaids, she glanced at the campfire and saw the space was empty. Whoever that man was and whatever his problem had been, it was no longer the concern of Caiaphas' household.

All day, Ruchel wondered about the meal her mother and sisters were most certainly preparing, even at that moment. Most servants were dismissed early on the day before the Passover to celebrate with their families. But that was only if all the work was finished, every iota of it. The food completed and ready to plate. The bedrooms all made up. Every speck of dust brushed from the furniture. All the mats and reclining couches in place. Pillows plumped. Every whim satisfied.

She had to smile as she thought about her mother's worries. *Would the lamb from Zakor be slaughtered on time at the Temple, so she'd have enough time to roast it before the evening meal? Was there enough wine? Would there be any last-minute visitors?*

Last year her brother, Zedekiah, had brought home a friend whose mother had been too ill to prepare the meal, and Ruchel had thought her mother would faint. He was finally seated after a flurry of moving chairs and finding plates and rearranging tableware.

What a tempest over something so small, she thought.

Ruchel pondered going home early, then having almost an entire day at home with her family to celebrate the Passover, plus the two additional days off she had been granted. What a luxury! Even on Sabbaths, she was often required to stay to tend the household if there were important guests. But on this Passover eve, the great Caiaphas would have to serve himself. She would sleep and bathe, washing her hair thoroughly for the first time in many weeks. She would visit her cousins and watch Elkanah painfully try to flirt with her. *It's a bit of fun to toy with him,* she thought with a wicked grin.

The early afternoon found Ruchel finishing up her tasks, even finding a little time to help Abigail sluice out the dairy. As she gathered her cloak and sack from the kitchen, she was surprised to find the cook beckoning to her by the fire.

"I've put a little away for you girls to take home to your families," she whispered, her wizened face creasing into dozens of lines as she grinned. The old woman held out a large chunk of a crumbly, golden cake. Ruchel knew it was made with rare blood oranges and potato starch, which took the place of flour during the Passover. The delicious smell made her want to grab the cake and take a bite right then and there, but she knew how delighted her family would be to have a taste.

Placing the cake carefully in her bag, Ruchel headed through the gateway of the compound. It was like entering another world when she crossed the threshold: Scribes hurrying toward the Temple, housemaids struggling with bags of vegetables, young boys scrapping together over a ball.

She was free, at least for a little while. She would take her time walking home in the spring sunshine. Ruchel's heart soared, and she began to hum a song she had learned as a child, then opened her mouth and began to sing:

"The Lord is in His Temple,
All within keep silence,
The Lord is on His throne,
All the world break into song ... "

A woman holding the hand of a small boy looked at her and smiled. She knew this young girl was celebrating the holiday, a day of liberation for her people, a day when Yahweh cast off the yoke of the Egyptians.

Ruchel decided she would take the long way home, around the back of the Temple, which would be booming with the grisly business of killing lambs and goats for families to roast. But the back of that courtyard bordered a lovely grove, and she wanted to stroll through it. When else would she have time on her own to enjoy the green leaves?

As she neared the courts of sacrifice, she could hear the panicked bleating of the lambs, could smell manure and blood and fear. *What a horrible job*, she thought, *to have to slaughter animals all day long.* Because she was a woman, she could never be part of the actual killing, which was fine with her. Only the circumcised and those clean before the Law could participate. Her brother had described it to her:

The animal was killed by an expert, someone who would make sure the creature didn't suffer. A priest would catch the blood in a cup with a rounded bottom so it could not sit down upon the ground. That priest would hand the cup to the next priest, so there was a relay line to the altar, with the last priest sprinkling the blood onto the altar.

Then the animal was hung on special hooks or sticks and skinned, with the abdomen cut open and the fatty portions placed in a vessel, salted, and offered by the priest on the altar. Finally, the lamb was ready to bring home to the spit, where it would be roasted and eaten. Ruchel had never thought much about these commands of Moses. They were simply as much a part of her life as her family or the path she walked to work each day. When you didn't look at it, you didn't notice it. She only knew that a taste of lamb once each year was a treat.

But today, Ruchel began to feel ill as she came upon the vendors outside the Temple, shouting loudly to catch the attention of passersby; the money changers who preyed on those coming to make offerings; the agitated herd of lambs in a nearby pen, waiting their turn for slaughter. She put a hand to her forehead, willing the dizzying nausea to pass.

What is wrong with me? she wondered. *Could it be something I ate for lunch? Please, please don't let me be ill over my few days with my family.* Sweat broke out between her breasts and down the back of her neck. Her hair suddenly felt extraordinarily heavy and so, so hot as the sun—a strange sun that seemed shrouded behind dark clouds but threw off a grayish miasma of light—gave the whole world a look of twilight. Ruchel staggered to a bench next to a vendor selling doves for sacrifice, letting her head drop low and dragging her bag on the dusty path in front of her.

Something was definitely wrong with her. The pen of lambs seemed to move closer and closer as she clutched her stomach.

Perfect lambs, without blemish or spot ...

The metallic smell of hot blood and entrails assaulted her nostrils, making her gag.

... he was led like a lamb to the slaughter ...

She felt bile rise in her throat and knew she was going to vomit.

... as a sheep before its shearers is silent ...

And the sound—the clamor—it was driving itself into her head. She gripped her temples between her hands.

All who see me mock me; they hurl insults ...

"What is happening to me?" Ruchel gasped, clutching the sides of the bench, trying to right herself in the whirling landscape. A woman from the dove stall bent beside her.

"Girl, are you all right?"

Ruchel winced in pain at the woman's touch. "I don't know," she whispered. "I'm so ... sick. What time is it?" Surely her mother would be waiting for her. She needed to go home.

"It's nearly the ninth hour," the woman replied. "Can I get you some water?"

Ruchel pushed the woman's hand away and lurched up from the bench. Leaving her bag in the dust under the seat, she staggered down the lane, clutching her stomach, the woman looking after her in disgust. *Probably drunk,* she thought.

When she'd moved far away from the courtyard, Ruchel finally stopped long enough to lean on a corner building, her hands running back and forth over the rough stones. Only then did she lean forward and retch, her throat hot and stinging. Her sickness lasted for several minutes until she was hollowed out, empty.

Wiping her mouth with her hand and wishing she had something to take away the sour taste, she stood up straight. The dizziness had passed. A cool breeze ruffled her hair. A cold sweat lingered on the back of her neck.

Ruchel knew one thing: She would never be able to eat lamb again.

www.ingramcontent.com/pod-product-compliance
Lightning Source LLC
Chambersburg PA
CBHW060317260626
47160CB00007B/2644